PRAISE FOR *A STRANG*

"Unimaginable evil stalks the dark, labyrinthian streets in the Greek Quarter of Victorian Odessa. Meanwhile another haunts the eerie catacombs below. Only the Karadopoulinas twin sisters can solve the string of grisly murders that have terrorized the city—but they'll have to stop sparring with each other first and work together as a team.

"A delightful and gripping Gothic murder mystery with a pair of humorous, courageous and refreshingly different young sleuths."

—Karen Charlton, author of *The Detective Lavender Mysteries* series

"A rollicking gothic-horror comedy magically set in 1900 Odessa."

—Judith Cutler, author of the *Harriet and Matthew Rowsley* series

"As dark and labyrinthine as the tunnels beneath Odessa, and with as many twists. Enthralling!"

—Clio Gray, author of Booker Nominated & Bailey's Longlisted *The Anatomist's Dream*

"A sly, wry look at murder, William Burton McCormick has given us the perfect read for Halloween—and the whole year. With a pair of quip-trading twins for sleuths, enough red herrings to fill a lake in Odessa, and a villain you won't readily guess, A Stranger from the Storm gives the reader a fast, snappy tour of times gone by in a place laden with history and secrets kept far underground."

—Jenny Milchman, USA Today bestselling author of *Cover of Snow* and *The Second Mother*

# A Stranger from the Storm

## William Burton McCormick

MANNISON PRESS, LLC
FLORIDA | NEW YORK

First Edition 2021
Published by Mannison Press, LLC
ISBN: 9798468942307

Cover design by Deidre J Owen © 2021 | deidrejowen.com
Editing by Morgan Schafer at Mannison Press, LLC
Interior design by Deidre J Owen

Visit mannisonpress.com.

In Memorium

Adrienne McCormick
and
Shawn McCormick

# CONTENTS

Odessa

"City of traditions, legends and memories,
City of spirits, ghosts and visions,
City of mines, catacombs and caves…"

*José de Ribas (1749–1800)*
*Spanish adventurer, Russian admiral,*
*and founder of modern Odessa*

# 1. Whistles in the Night

"Tasia, do you hear whistling?"

"No."

Fifteen-year-old Tasia looked up from her reading; her sister, Eleni, stood across the room peering through the opened front door into the darkened street beyond.

"Someone is whistling outside."

"It's the wind. Close the door, you're letting in rain."

Eleni ignored her. As usual. *Why even speak?*

Instead, Tasia returned her attention to the printed journal in hand. On the front of the English Club's newsletter was the review of their lodging house:

# A Grand Stay
# In the Greek Quarter

All well and good. But on the back of the same page was the tempting coupon for a drafting and drawing correspondence course from London. Tasia angled the scissors carefully. No matter how much Mother wanted to save the article, a twenty percent discount was a twenty percent discount.

Tasia licked her lips. If she could just trim enough to cut out the coupon, Mother would be none the wiser. A bit of margin missing, some trailing punctuation lost...

There.

Tasia put down the scissors, flipped back to the front.

Hmm...

# A Gran
# In the Gree

Sounds like Welsh.

"Tasia, come here!" her sister shouted.

With a few mutterings, Tasia rose from her chair and joined Eleni at the door. Though slightly younger, her sister was taller and blessed with a more womanly shape (a point of great and undeserved pride in Eleni, Tasia thought). Well, appearances aside, Tasia *was* the elder sibling and she squeezed in front of her sister at the threshold.

"What is it?"

"I told you someone was whistling."

"At this hour?" Tasia squinted into the darkness. The passing storm had blown out the gas lamps and cleared the streets of traffic; now all was still save a light rain rippling through the puddles. In the haze, Tasia could see the glazed silhouette of a man walking to and fro along the opposite side of the street, a tuneless whistle carrying with him.

The deep soundings of the distant cathedral clock told Tasia it was midnight on the hour.

"What's he doing?" asked Eleni.

Tasia watched the figure a moment. The man would take a few steps one way, then turn about and go the other, all the time staring intensely at the building facade above him.

"He's looking for a street number."

"He must be a desperate fool to be out in this weather, Tasia."

"So's Mother."

"My point exactly."

Lightning branched through the Black Sea sky, dark clouds glowing like oven coals above. The rumbling came a moment later, the man's whistle drowned out by deep sea thunder.

His attention turned their way. Tasia pulled the door closer.

Something in his posture told her that he'd seen them; the man quickly crossed the street, a lurch in his step as he trampled through the flooded gutter.

"I'll bet you a week of chores he's a foreigner," whispered Eleni. "He doesn't walk right."

"A limp's not national."

"You'll see."

Tasia hushed her sister, felt her stomach knotting in apprehension. Strangers calling so late made her nervous, especially with Mother absent. Especially with that fiend prowling the Slavic Quarter. She gritted her teeth. Still, they could use the money.

As he passed in range of the house lamps, their visitor came slowly into focus. A tall fellow dressed in a dark overcoat, he had a roundish face with thick white curls sprouting beneath a pleated cap, the tangled hairs trailing down his cheeks into bushy sideburns. There was something reflective in those cheeks that caught the light, casting a faint halo about his face as he approached.

The man slowed at the doorstep, seemingly slightly befuddled. "Do you speak English?"

"We both do," Tasia said, ignoring the victorious nudge from Eleni.

"Excellent." He nodded towards the sign in the window. "I see you have a room to let. May I?"

"Of course." Tasia ushered the man inside, pushing her sister back to give their visitor room. He was thoroughly drenched and carried an odor of summer sweat with him. As he hurried up the steps, Tasia could see his limp was more pronounced than she'd thought.

"Are you injured?"

"I turned my ankle on these mud troughs you call streets." He grimaced. "I'll elevate it tonight to keep the blood from it."

Such a thick, throaty voice, she thought. English or Scottish perhaps? Certainly not Welsh…it was so hard to know their accents.

Inside their parlor, Tasia lit the oil lamps to take a better look at their guest. He seemed about fifty, more than a little worn, with the thick hands of a working man. But as he turned towards her, Tasia felt her eyes widen in horror. From each corner of his mouth stretched a wide scar reaching nearly to his ears, a ridge of pink-white skin cutting through his sideburns in the hideous facsimile of a smile. Tasia was at a loss for words.

But her sister wasn't: "That seems painful."

"Eleni!"

She shrugged. "Well, it does look painful."

Their guest was not amused. "It was excruciating, young lady. And if I'd opened my mouth to scream my face would have split apart." He shook the rainwater from his cap. "Fortunately, I'm not a man who screams."

He kept an eye on Eleni. "Are you a woman who screams?"

"No."

"Good. Some do." He hung his cap on the hat peg. "Now, who should I speak with about a room?"

Tasia stepped forward, still unnerved. "You can talk to me. I'm the eldest."

"Ah, but you look about the same."

"I'm a day older."

"A day?"

"Yes." Tasia brushed the creases from her skirt. *To business…* "We can't actually—formally—give you the room until Mother returns. Her rules, you know. But you can wait in here until she arrives. It won't be long."

"At this hour, I should hope not." He wandered towards the rear of their parlor, taking in the warmth of the little room. "Are there any other lodgers?"

Out of the corner of her eye, Tasia saw Eleni earnestly mouthing "Yes, yes. Say 'yes'" behind him.

"No," she said, enjoying Eleni's reaction. "At present you have the full choice of rooms."

He snorted. "Well, let's have a look then." Without hesitation, he opened the door to the room beneath the stairs and disappeared inside.

"Be our guest," snapped Eleni, exchanging surprised glances with Tasia.

Tasia trailed the man to the doorway, unsure she wanted to follow further. The bedroom beyond was the largest in their house, which meant it was the smallest in most homes: A floor of uneven boards without a rug, a thin bed smothered beneath a Tartan quilt in the corner and nearby, a dwarf-sized door to the only private bath they had. And in the center of the far wall was a grand storm window complete with cushioned sitting step and flowered oriental curtains, the house lamps shimmering through the pane to cast fairy sparks off the wet stones of the courtyard beyond.

Tasia caught her reflection in the glass. She looked nervous and young.

"This will be perfect," he said with clear satisfaction.

Locking her arm around Eleni's, Tasia reluctantly stepped inside. "The ones upstairs are cooler in summer."

"No. This is the one I want. How much for a fortnight?"

"Again, Mother does—"

"I thought you were the eldest?"

"As the eldest, I obey the rules. And it might be best if you waited in the—"

"Certainly." He sat down on the bed and began to fiddle with the strings on his boots. "We can discuss this in the morning."

"Sir, if I could ask—"

"Look at this," he said with disgust. "The laces are fraying and the leather is coming apart. If I'd known your streets were torrid rivers, I'd have brought a pair of Wellingtons."

"You are English, then?"

"A Londoner." He pushed the boot off his swollen ankle, the sole landing with a wet plop on their slanted floor. The man let out a great sigh, smiling briefly. "How is it you both speak the Queen's language?"

"Mother has—had—friends in the mining industry. Our house is filled with Welshmen every season on their way to and from the coal camps near Hughesovka."

"Has been since we were babies," added Eleni.

"Well, if you learned the English language from Welsh miners it's a miracle you can speak a word."

Eleni crossed her arms, spat out: *"Twll dîn pob Sais."*

Their guest scowled at this remark, returning such a hard stare over that jack-o-lantern grin that Eleni's face drained of all color. "I'd be careful, my rude young Miss, I've spent enough time in Pontypridd to know the less flattering Welsh phrases. You could lose more than a lodger should you persist."

There were several moments of stunned silence before Tasia found her wits. "I'm sure my sister simply mispronounced something more complimentary," she said, ushering Eleni out the door. "We'll let you rest undisturbed until Mother arrives."

"A wise choice."

Tasia shut the door behind them. "Are you mad, Eleni?"

"I think he just threatened me."

"No. He's simply angry because you keep insulting him. Really, where are your manners?"

"My manners close at ten o'clock. After that, you get what you get." She marched over to the chair near the lamp and took a seat. "He should be thanking us. In this weather? At midnight? With that scar? He's lucky we ever opened the door."

"You could be a better hostess."

"Well, perhaps it's because I'm the baby?" She rolled her eyes. "'A day older?' I'm tired of hearing you say that every time we have a guest."

"Well, it's true." Tasia pointed up the stairs. "Go look at the certificates in Mother's letter desk. 'Anastasia Ioannou Karadopoulina born 21 September 1884. Eleni Ioannou Karadopoulina born 22 September 1884.' One day's difference."

"Just because Mother had you at a quarter to midnight and me at five after."

"Oh, and what a day it was…a marvelous Sunday." Tasia laughed, twirling the violet ribbon in her hair. "If you'd only been born on the Sabbath like me, instead of being a dreary Monday baby."

"Monday's when work is done, not that you'd—"

That husky foreign voice boomed from behind the backroom door. "Ladies, could you cease your shouting? It is the dead of night after all."

"Certainly, Mister... Mister...?" Tasia lowered her voice to a whisper. "I don't even know his name."

"He hasn't paid a kopek and he's telling us what to do." Eleni propped her chin in her palm. "A peculiar fellow in every way."

Tasia shrugged. "He's English. They're all like that. World-spanning Empire and such."

Eleni stared at that closed door for several moments, a pensive look on her face. "You know, Tasia, he has no bags."

"Yes...peculiar."

"That word keeps cropping up, doesn't it?"

There was the click of a latch and the welcome rush of fresh air as the front door opened. Mother stepped wearily inside, a frail, curly-haired lady with far too many lines in her face for forty. Soaked to the bone, her dress hung limply from a tiny frame as she fought to close her stubborn umbrella. The way she let their "Room to Let" sign slip to the floor, Tasia knew exactly how things had gone at the harbor.

"Mother," Tasia said, smiling. "We've good news."

"Are you both all right? You haven't been out, have you?" Her face was white as the seawall.

"We're fine, Mother."

"What's wrong, Mama?" asked Eleni, rising from her chair.

"Didn't you hear the whistles?"

Tasia glanced at her sister. "Whistles? We only heard—"

"Police whistles." Mother fastened the door bolts, heavy metallic clanks as she made sure they were secure. "There was a murder, not an hour ago."

# 2. Murder and Mr. Humble

"Another murder?" gasped Eleni.

Mother nodded as she took a seat near the window. "On Avchinnikov Lane in the Slavic Quarter."

"That's not four blocks from here."

At the back of the room, Tasia turned up the lamps, chasing grim shadows to the corners. It did little to lighten her mood. "Was it the Specter?"

"I don't know, probably. It was an infant this time." Mother placed a hand to her temple, clearly drained by the ordeal. "I was coming up Yevreiskaya Street and there was a crowd gathering at the entrance to Avchinnikov. It's just a little side street, and the police were keeping everyone back. It must have happened only minutes before." Mother took a slow breath to calm herself. "I ran into Mrs. Tabatskaya, she'd been there since the first whistle."

Eleni knelt beside Mother, gently taking her hand. "What did she say? Do they know anything?"

"The baby's mother walked in on the killer in the nursery, found him smothering her child in his arms. Oh, it would be horrible." She looked over to Tasia, still lingering at the back. "I guess the mother screamed and the fiend dropped the infant dead to the floor and fled out the window. The monster fell a full story to the alley and disappeared into the storm."

Tasia glanced at her sister. "Poor woman, can you imagine?"

"Did she get a good look at him?"

"Mrs. Tabatskaya couldn't say. The mother must be hysterical."

Tasia suppressed a shudder. "It's hard to believe something like this could happen so close to home."

"They've penned off the streets to the Slavic Quarter." Mother caressed Eleni's cheek as if to reassure herself that her own children were safe. "Have you seen Spiro?"

"No, Mother. His shift ends at dawn."

Something half-remembered stirred in Tasia's mind. "We've a lodger, Mother. An Englishman."

"A lodger?"

"In the large bedroom."

"Really?" She smiled weakly, welcoming the change of topic. "Well, that is a turn of fortune." Mother rose from her chair. "What time did he arrive?"

"About midnight."

"He's got a hideous scar, Mama," whispered Eleni.

Mother arranged her drenched hair, peering into the looking glass perched on the bookshelf. "Eleni, it's not the body that matters but the soul."

"Well, his soul better be pretty good."

With an unsatisfied mumble, Mother finished at the mirror and walked to the door beneath the stairs. She pressed an ear gently against it. "Is he still awake?" She glanced back at her daughters. They shrugged.

"Has he paid?"

Tasia shrugged again. "I didn't know what you wanted to charge him, Mother." She dropped her voice to a murmur. "He *is* English."

Mother considered this a moment, gave a cerebral nod, then knocked on the door with three quick, professional raps.

The reply was immediate: "Enter."

Mother opened the door, their lodger visible inside. He did not repose on the bed as Tasia expected, but instead sat on the cushioned seat at the window, his bad foot propped on a stool. He'd placed the room's oil lamp on the floor nearby, Mother's shadow stretching across a brightened floor, the ceiling receding into darkness.

"Forgive me for not rising, Madame, but my ankle seems to be stiffening."

"Of course." There was a hesitance in Mother's voice. Standing behind, Tasia could not see her face, yet imagined the reaction. The adult, professional veneer painting over the horror. *The scar, Mother. We warned you…*

"I'm Maia Karadopoulina, proprietor. Do you need help with the foot?"

"None required. Thank you."

Tasia came around to Mother's side, gaining a clearer view of their new tenant. He had thrown his overcoat over the bedpost and sat in a gray and threadbare waistcoat, a loosened avocado necktie the only decoration. Across his knee lay a leather-bound journal, a worn pencil in his left hand. The lamp underfoot reversed the shadows on his face, pooling light in the recesses of his brow and under his chin. Tasia thought of children playing at ghost tales over the fire. It did little to hide the scar, she thought, a ghastly white smile stretching through the darkness.

"Do you like the room?" asked Mother, her voice a bit more composed.

"Yes, it's fine." He tapped a finger on the window glass. "Though I have to ask: Does this pane open wider?"

"No. It's a ground floor window. That's as far as it goes."

"A pity. We could use more breeze." He made a little note in his book.

"I am sorry for the late hour interruption."

"I overheard a commotion through these rather thin walls." He cocked his head curiously. "Has there been a problem?"

"You mean the storm?"

"I mean the death." He shut the journal. "Was it the same fellow who killed the Poliakoff boy last month?"

Mother clearly didn't like this subject. "I don't know, but it seems likely. There have been five murders this summer."

"Six, Mother," corrected Tasia. "After tonight."

"Yes, six."

"It's the Specter," blurted out Eleni from the doorway, more than a little thrill in her voice.

"The Specter?"

Mother crossed her arms about her shoulders as if fighting a chill. "Some fellow has been writing to the newspapers claiming he is the murderer. I don't follow such rubbish, but I guess he calls himself 'The Specter.'"

"How melodramatic."

"You've no concern. Nothing's happened in this part of town. And the devil seems to be only after children."

He glanced out the window. "Well, we shouldn't feel too safe and cozy. An unsettled mind may seek new challenges, don't you think?"

"That's why we bolt the doors, Mister…"

"Mr. Henry Humble, at your service." He turned back towards Mother. "It's rather fortunate that you speak English. My Russian is very weak."

Mother added a welcome authority to her tone that made Tasia smile. "You won't find much Russian spoken in this house, Mr. Humble. You're in the Greek Quarter."

He laughed. "Really? I must have been spun topsy-turvy in the storm."

"Do you still want the room?"

"Why not?" He set the journal on the windowsill. "It seems fate has swept me into a friendly harbor."

"Just the night then?"

"For a whole fortnight at least. I've come off an exceedingly long tour." He donned a warm smile. "I'm a navigator on commercial vessels out of Tilbury. Thought I'd spend some of this year on land. I've heard Odessa is wonderful in summer."

"It's two rubles per week."

"A bargain."

*And twice what others pay.* Tasia laughed to herself. Perhaps, this old Englishman wasn't so fearsome after all. She whispered to Eleni, who had crept up to her shoulder, "He's so much sweeter to Mother, isn't he?"

"Maybe he fancies her. What kind of name is 'Henry?'"

"One of their kings."

"What'd he do?"

"Killed all his wives."

"Oh my!"

Mother glanced their way. For a moment Tasia feared she'd heard the remarks, but her distant gaze seemed to be searching the room.

Mother returned her attention to their guest. "Don't you have bags, Mr. Humble?"

"They're still aboard ship. I'll fetch them tomorrow."

"With your ankle, my daughters can get them for you."

"That won't be necessary."

She seemed to consider him a moment, then finally: "All right, well, if you're going to have an extended stay, here are the rules."

"The rules?"

"No weapons and no drunkenness. And no guests after ten o'clock."

"Agreeable enough."

"You'll have a key to your room and the main. But I latch the second bolt at twelve midnight and don't open it again until five. If you're out during those hours, you stay out. Don't come knockin' at my window, you'll get no answer."

He nodded silently.

"Are you a married man, Mr. Humble?"

"My wife is deceased."

"Those Henrys again…" muttered Eleni.

"You have our sympathies," said Mother. "I lost a husband myself. There's nothing more terrible to a soul, except the death of a child, I suppose."

"Yes, well, it was a suicide. And the world is better rid of her, I think."

Tasia looked to Eleni whose eyes were wide as saucers. Tasia half-expected Mother to show Mr. Humble, his bad leg, and ugly smile the door, but instead she composed herself and continued.

"Yes, well…all sympathies aside…" She let out a breath. "As my daughters are coming of age, they're not here for courting. They're here for housekeep and the odd errand. We act and speak decently around them. Any lodger of ours must respect that he's living in a house with unmarried girls."

He let his eyes linger over Eleni. "I've no romantic interest in your daughters, Mrs. Karadopoulina."

"I didn't expect that you did." She clasped her hands together in greeting. "Now that we've finished the rules, let us welcome you to our home. I've run a boarding house near twenty years. Many of our lodgers are like family."

"Then why is your house empty?"

Mother's eyes narrowed. "These are difficult times, Mr. Humble." She ushered her daughters out. "You can pay in the morning. I'll bid you goodnight."

"Kalinikta," said Tasia as she exited, not in the mood for stuffy English.

"Nos da," added Eleni with a saintly smile.

Mr. Humble gave a cough. "Ah, Mrs. Karadopoulina…I have one last question." He pointed to an off-color section of the floor near the bath door. "Why do those boards bow like that?"

"I'm afraid my late husband wasn't much of a carpenter." Mother motioned around the room with her hand. "This is an old patrician house and that space led down to a leaky half-cellar. It was too small to put a bed in and not much use in a boarding house, so we sealed it up when we acquired the property."

"And it has remained undisturbed all this time?"

She frowned. "I helped my husband nail in those boards, Mr. Humble. They haven't been moved in nineteen years."

This seemed to give him some satisfaction. "Thank you, Mrs. Karadopoulina. I was simply curious." He gave her a gentle nod. "Goodnight."

# 3. A Sporting Man

*So you think you nearly had me last night? That I was pinned down in Slavic Town, tail between my legs? Well, I'm not afraid to wander, dear friends. And as a sporting man, I'll even give you a hint. On 17 July I'll kill a brat in every quarter of this city.*

*Try and stop me,*
*The Specter*

(Letter received by the Odessa newspaper *Southern Review* on 10 July 1900.)

# 4. Snapping Twigs

"Play the music, Tasia, not simply the notes."

"Yes, Mr. Telidis." She smiled sheepishly as she reset her fingers to the proper positions on the piano. "I'm sorry."

Tasia resumed her practice of "Souvenir de Vienne," tapping at the keys without much heart. Her mind simply wasn't on her lessons, the source of distraction clearly visible through the window at her shoulder. Across the courtyard stood their lodging house, their new friend Mr. Humble sitting in the window of his room reading a newspaper and smoking a cigar. The aligned windows framed Mr. Humble so perfectly that he seemed a painting hung on the wall, his presence smothering her passion for music. An anti-muse who would never go away.

"Tasia, you've lost both tempo and tune. Must we start again?"

"I'll get it, Mr. Telidis," She said, frustration growing in her voice. "Forgive me."

She sat in the house of Gregorios Telidis: neighbor, family friend, and Tasia's occasional music teacher. A cheerful man who insisted his students call him "Gregorios" or even "Gregori," though Tasia could never be so informal with a tutor. Mr. Telidis was a young Greek, not yet thirty, but in manner and dress he seemed ages older than Mother, a dusty heirloom from some bygone era.

"What is the matter with you today, Tasia?" said Mr. Telidis, rubbing his chin whiskers to appear the stern tutor. But then the mask crumbled and he broke out in a smile. "I think it is the heat. Lemonade would help your concentration."

"That would be wonderful. Thank you."

She watched him rise from his stool to fetch the pitcher. A bit of a shame, she thought, that he dressed so old fashioned. Mr. Telidis would actually be handsome if his spectacles didn't turn his eyes to glassy orbs, and if he'd discarded the odd-looking belt he wore, the Bulgarian one that stretched halfway to his ribs. It made him the butt of jokes the neighborhood round. "Leather belly" the crueler children called him.

Mr. Telidis filled two glasses, mixing in an extra helping of sugar for her. His detractors were mistaken; Mr. Telidis was terribly kind to those who knew him, almost too much so. When Mother could no longer afford the lessons, he'd continued her tutoring for free because Tasia was "so gifted."

She plinked a piano key. That too must be a joke.

Tasia looked back out the window hoping for a sunny day. But there was only Mr. Humble turning the page of his newspaper. Though she couldn't read the print at this distance, she could see the headlines were written in Cyrillic characters.

*I thought your Russian was poor, Mr. Humble…*

"Mr. Telidis, how long have I been your pupil?"

"Near two years, I think."

"Can I confide in you?"

He sat down on the piano stool next to Tasia, handed her a glass. "Of course, though if this is going to be some story of tortured young love, I'm afraid I can't be of much assistance." He laughed. "Like all men, I'm a complete dunce in affairs of the heart."

Tasia smiled. "Nothing of that sort." She nodded towards the window. "There's something odd about our new lodger, Mr. Humble."

He took a sip of the lemonade. "What is it you find strange?"

"Many things. He's out all night, it seems. Nearly every time Mother unlocks the door in the morning, there he is, sitting on the step. Eleni calls him our 'housecat,' always waiting to be let in."

Mr. Telidis chuckled, something knowing in the laughter. "He's a seaman ashore. You don't expect him to spend his nights at home, do you?"

*Yes, well...* "And he's only going to be here for a few weeks, yet yesterday he bought a Turkish rug for his floor. I helped him unroll it myself—without receiving a thank you, I might add." She scowled at the memory. "It's thicker, better quality than any in the house. He must have paid a fortune."

"Maybe he's a wealthy man."

"He doesn't dress like it. His clothes are stained and fraying. His wardrobe is worse than mine."

"We can only hope his musicianship is better."

"Mr. Telidis..." She tasted a bit of lemonade—too sugary. "Did I deserve that?"

"Concentration, Tasia." He pointed to his temple. "It's a quality all artists share. One must be totally focused on one's work for it to develop. A trait you most certainly lack."

"Yes, Mr. Telidis."

"Gregorios."

She realized how close he was sitting to her. "'Mr. Telidis.'" She smiled. "Until I turn seventeen at least."

"A difficult age."

"I wouldn't know."

He watched her a moment, spry summer light reflecting off his glasses. Finally, a breath. "Well, let me put your mind at ease." He rose from the stool. "I can say that I think your Mr. Humble is a very agreeable fellow."

"You've met him?"

"Yes. He's come over twice just to say 'Hello.' Making the neighborhood rounds, I guess. We shared some tobacco, talked about music and the sea. He told me all about his adventures in Afghanistan. Wonderful tales. A friendly man, as foreigners go."

"He never says a word to us."

"Perhaps he can sense your discomfort around him. Is it his disfigurement that you find disconcerting? I would hope you would be better than that, Tasia."

She glanced back across the courtyard, found Mr. Humble in his window. Never a wave or acknowledgement, just reading. But always there.

"Yes, I guess I should be."

Krek.

Krek.

*What is that?*

Krek.

*It sounds like snapping twigs.*

Krek.

Krek.

*Snapping twigs, in the house?*

Tasia rolled over to her sister's side of the bed. "Eleni, do you hear that?"

No answer. She lay fast asleep, head comfortably sunk into a deep feather pillow.

Tasia's eyes darted about their darkened room. A moonless night, she could see nothing beyond the end of the bed, not even her own reflection on the mirror near the wall.

A moment passed. No further sounds. She hadn't dreamt it, had she? It was always the quiet that scared

Tasia the most, the breathless stillness waiting for confirmation—

Krek, krek…

*Oh, God, it's real…* Tasia shook her sister. "Eleni, please!"

She rolled away. "Kiss me again, Spiro. Mother's not home…"

"Eleni!"

She rubbed her face, eyes slowly opening. "Tasia…I was sleeping."

"There's a sound downstairs."

"A sound?"

"Listen."

Eleni hesitated. "All I hear is the clock. You're imagining—"

A faint cracking, far below.

Eleni sat up to an elbow. "What is that?"

Tasia swung her legs over the bedside. "It's like splitting wood." She lit the lamp by the bed, their shadows stretching up the slanted walls of the little attic bedroom.

"Maybe somebody's making kindling?"

"At this hour? In July?" Tasia lifted the lamp from the nightstand. "We're going downstairs."

"We?"

Tasia gave Eleni her cruelest stare, the one copied directly from Mother.

"All right, 'we.'"

Barefoot on the sticky floor of summer, Tasia slipped out the door of their room, Eleni trailing behind. Quietly, they climbed down the narrow steps onto the cramped and humid landing, the doorways on either side open and dark, Mother's in the center shut tight for the night.

"Should we wake her?" asked Eleni.

Tasia put a finger to her lips. "Listen."

The noises repeated, echoing up from the ground floor.

"That's not natural."

"No its not," whispered Tasia, a chill running down her spine. She pooled her courage, taking her sister's hand. "We do this together."

Eleni nodded. "All right."

Lantern stretched out ahead of them, they descended to the ground floor. *This is our home,* Tasia reminded herself. *Nothing to be afraid of. It's simply some sound of city life—*

Krek…krek…

Tasia winced. *Well, maybe…*

As she stepped down into the parlor, Tasia found the source. It was as she suspected, even feared. She held up the lamp, a yellow spotlight on the little door. The noises were emanating from the bedroom beneath the stairs.

"Well, there's a surprise," growled Eleni. "The housecat is clawing at the furniture."

"We don't know that, it could be…"

"Could be what? Termites?" Eleni caught herself. "Or death watch beetles burrowing through the wood."

"Just a superstition."

"Maybe. Mama heard them the night Papa died."

"This is no insect." Tasia rapped lightly on the door. "Mr. Humble, are you in there?"

Silence.

She knocked again, a bit louder this time. "Mr. Humble?"

There was a rustle, then heavy footsteps on the floor. The door flashed open, a sneering Mr. Humble standing behind it in his open-breasted night robe; a briar of salt and pepper chest hairs and the smell of camphor oil sending Tasia a step back.

"What is it?"

"What were you doing in there?" asked Tasia, surprised by the strength in her voice. "We heard cracking."

He rolled his eyes. "If anything, you heard creaking. I was trying to compose a letter and did a bit of pacing about the room."

"Show us," demanded Eleni.

Mr. Humble looked at them a moment, then released a sigh. "If you must come in, you must."

He stepped back and allowed Tasia to shine the lamp inside. With the window curtains drawn and the courtyard dark, their lonely light seemed a mere candle flame as she shone it around the room. All looked normal: the unmade bed remained intact, as was the dresser against the wall, and the footstool in the corner; the lamp's soft glow casting a watery reflection over the room's polished floorboards, that stiff new rug a dark island in the center.

Tasia withdrew the lamp. Nothing appeared amiss. "Satisfied?"

Tasia glanced at Eleni who only shrugged. "I suppose."

"Good. As it is"—he squinted in the direction of the dresser clock—"nearly half three, I should think I would be entitled to some privacy. If you bother me again, I will insist your mother refund my monies for this night."

"Oh…" Tasia's stomach knotted at the thought. That would be most unpleasant.

"Should I fetch Mother?"

"No."

"Then goodnight." And he shut the door.

# 5. The Watcher in Darkness

"Oxygen debt?" asked Tasia.

"Oxygen debt," answered Eleni, and she dove into the swimming hole.

Sitting on the stones above, Tasia watched her sister disappear beneath black waters. Barely a ripple at entry and Eleni was transformed into a glaze of red and white along the bottom; a ghost gliding beneath the feet of every child splashing at the surface. With remarkable speed she reached the opposite side, reversing her course without rising, without breath. How comfortable Eleni was in the water. Tasia couldn't even swim.

But she had other skills. Tasia returned to her sketchbook, rendering the scene with colored chalks carefully selected from the tin beside her. This swimming hole, drawn in tans and greens, was just an old quarry filled with rainwater, an urban oasis one short trolley stop from home, and the gathering place of summer youth for blocks around.

Tasia switched to a softer chalk, lightly sketching in the details. Yellowy grass lived in the cracks of the edge-stones at her feet, while over her shoulders the white branches of acacias spread out above the waters, the thicker limbs adorned with sun-bleached ropes for fanny dunking. Over the treetops loomed the elegant balconies of handsome limestone buildings, the hallmark of Odessa's center. Here elderly couples sat hand-in-hand with grandchildren while cursing young wives pounded the dust from carpets and tanned carpenters musically sawed and sanded their wares for market. *The city on a shelf*, Tasia thought, and she titled her work the same.

Every summer Tasia captured this place on canvas and every summer she prayed it would remain untouched as Odessa grew. Thankfully, the Southern Wonder had land to spare, quarry-pools not yet the target of wealthy builders. Or so Mother said.

Tasia signed and dated her annual masterpiece. Maybe next year in oils?

Eleni swam up, clearly winded by her underwater excursion.

"I'll ask again," said Tasia. "What is oxygen debt?"

Eleni pressed her cheek lightly against the edge-stone, taking several moments to catch her breath. "Women who can go longer without air die less often in childbirth. Something about tolerating blood loss…it said so in the *Manchester Scientific Ledger,*" she said, referring to one of the numerous journals dragged home from their latest trip to the English Club. She pushed off again into the water. "I'm going to have a large family."

Tasia shook her head. Bizarre girl Eleni. How could they possibly be sisters?

Eleni backstroked to the center of the pool then rolled over and disappeared beneath the waters. Tasia counted the seconds silently, a full minute passing, then nearly two before Eleni broke the surface gasping, her face as red as her swimming dress.

*How ridiculous.* "And just how many children do you plan to have?"

Eleni took a few weak strokes to the quarry edge, clinging to the slick stones and looking faint. "Well, if Spiro proposes when I'm eighteen, we'll have our first child at nineteen." She closed her eyes, consciously trying to slow her breathing. "Then one every other year for the next fifteen years, the olders helping with the youngers, I'll—"

"Nine children? On his policeman's wage?" Tasia laughed and went back to her sketches. "And they say artists are naïve."

Eleni managed a smile on her flushed face. "Oh, Spiro doesn't just live off wages." She snickered between coughs. "He's got other ways to fill the dinner pot."

Tasia stared at her little sister for a moment, so cherub-red at the pool's edge. "Eleni…he doesn't 'close his eyes' for profit, does he? Like so many policemen do?"

"Now who's being naïve, Tasia?"

"Well?"

"How else to have a family?"

"Hello there!" shouted a familiar voice. As if summoned by his mentioning, Spiro emerged from the shade of the footpath across the quarry. Bare-chested and barefooted, he wore only a pair of white cotton trousers, picking his way over the slippery stones to find a seat at the waters' edge. He was a handsome Greek of twenty-two—though they told Mother only nineteen—broad shouldered and muscular, with curly dark hair and the blue-green eyes of the summer sea. Eyes for Eleni only, apparently.

"There he is." Eleni cast off towards the other side. "Don't say anything about children."

Tasia nodded. She had been a little jealous when Spiro started courting Eleni last autumn. It was impossible not to be with such a beautiful man making daily calls, saying little to Tasia, asking only if her sister was at home. Of course, now that Tasia knew he closed his eyes there wasn't such a loss. Perhaps Mother should know?

And perhaps that's why Spiro ignored their complaints about Mr. Humble?

Across the pool, Spiro waved an acknowledgement to Tasia and then leaned forward to talk with Eleni at the waterline. An intimate conversation in a pool full of children.

Tasia sighed. Well, what to do now? She really had no desire to be a witness to Eleni's latest romance. The sun was burning her neck and ankles and, yes, there were more interesting vistas to sketch in shadier parts of Odessa.

Putting on her shoes, Tasia packed up her things and made her way along the water's edge to a rocky spot where the trees were only stumps and the road passed close by. She slipped her chalk tin into her dress pocket, and pressing her sketchbook to her chest, climbed down into a stony inlet right above the waterline. It hid an entrance to an old mine, one of a few that dotted the perimeter of the quarry. Tasia had ducked in here many times waiting out summer rains or finding shade when the sun got too hot. A grid of iron bars set a few feet inside the hole theoretically barred exploration, but the barrier was not maintained, and some intrepid Odessan had dug out an opening beneath the lowest crossbar.

Tasia peered through the bars. The narrow tunnel ahead extended into gloom, a few rays of angled light breaking the darkness from sinkholes in the road above. It reminded her of the Catholic cathedral on Katernskaya Boulevard, the interior so long and dark compared to their Orthodox churches.

She would call her drawing "The Basilica."

Sketchbook in hand, Tasia crawled under the bar. The atmosphere inside was noticeably cooler, a musky scent swimming in the air. At her knees were fragments of bottle glass and cigarette butts, and farther in, the ashen stains of campfires. But these traces of trespassers dwindled as she pressed deeper, only the laughter of children in the pool carried with her, reminding Tasia how near civilization was.

She ran her fingertips along the coarse stone wall as she walked. These were the old limestone mines used to raise Odessa. Tasia wasn't really sure how far these passages went, some said they snaked under the entire city, exits turning up in the most unexpected of places: old closets, furnace rooms, abandoned fields.

But Tasia knew *this* tunnel. Well, at least the first twenty yards. The final ceiling hole was as far as she'd ventured, beyond that was nothing but unexplored darkness.

Tasia settled herself beneath the last of the sinkholes, the sunlight just enough to work with. The fissure above was small and Tasia could see little of the street level. A bit of a pink building through the break, some fat woman fanning herself in a window, birds circling in the distant sky.

Sitting in this natural spotlight, she turned to face the entrance. Now, how to sketch "The Basilica?" So many contrasts. This would be—

On the edge of the sunbeam something stirred. A pallid form creeping along the base of the wall, indistinct and fuzzy—until it hopped into the light.

A rabbit? Tasia started. It was a rabbit!

Ears twitching, nose wrinkling, the little speckled beast sniffed about in the spotlight ahead, shooting a few curious glances at Tasia, but it was seemingly unconcerned by her close proximity.

A rabbit in the city center? She sat amazed. A resident of Odessa's generous parks, no doubt, or some subterranean hare living forever in these mines. Tasia smiled. Or perhaps he was the scourge of some farmer's field having eloped through miles of tunnels to this point. Yes, she liked this; it fired her artist's imagination, as if she'd followed Alice through the looking glass or down the rabbit hole or whatever it was.

Tasia sketched the little creature into her picture, reciting to herself:

*"Twas brillig, and the slithy toves*
*Did gyre and gimble in the wabe;"*

The rabbit stared at her. Tasia wondered how well it could see and how keen were its other senses. Certainly, its sense of smell and hearing must surpass Man's.

*"All mimsy were the borogoves,*
*And the mome raths outgrabe."*

The rabbit grew deathly still. All the better to sketch him.

*"Beware the Jabberwock, my GIRL!*
*"The jaws that bite, the claws that catch!"*
*"Beware the—"*

The rabbit scurried down the passage, slipping under the bars of the exit.

"Well, goodbye," she said, disappointed. Tasia reached for the gum eraser in her tin. It was then she felt the presence, an un-beckoned electricity rising up her spine, raising the hairs on her neck. Turning her shoulders, she peered down the tunnel behind. Within the gloom, beyond the reach of sunlight, stood a man, watching her. No features visible, only a tall thin shape barely in sight.

"Who are you?" she said, her voice dry as an autumn leaf.

She received no answer.

"Well, speak," Tasia repeated, rising to her feet. "Answer me."

The figure remained still.

Eyes never leaving him, Tasia tried to collect her chalks, but her trembling hands could not fasten the lid.

"You stay there—I'll be going." She fumbled with the tin. *Why won't this go on?*

He took a step forward.

She fled, dropping everything to run faster.

It all happened so quickly. The tunnel walls sped past, she was under the crossbar, and down somehow into the water. Her head plunged under first, the screams and footsteps and children's voices silenced, everything lost under white bubbling explosions as her breath sought the surface. Tasia flailed about, horrified to find herself half-upside down in a weightless world she couldn't navigate. Her motions spun her around, glimpses of light, darkness, the kicking legs of nearby children. Her extended arms sought the quarry edge, but these clumsy attempts sent her lower, toes and knees dragging in the silt at the bottom. The dirt rose up around her, eclipsing everything, invading her sinuses. She began to gag, water rushing into her lungs.

Her panic ebbing, she found it a cruel irony. To drown ten feet from the shore, surrounded by able children, all younger than she. Why had she never learned to swim? It serves you right, Tasia, you fool.

A figure appeared inside the cloudy water above. A swimmer fast approaching.

Eleni…

The great darkness of her eyes, the black-red of her swimming dress contrasting with pale face and limbs. A sheath of spinning bubbles around her, she seemed a ghastly figure, a Nightmare emerging from the stormy sky.

She would tell Eleni this in the afterworld; say that all her sister's beauty reminded Tasia only of illness, of death, and the grave. Of Father's last days in that bed.

She sank lower, below Eleni's grip.

Then a man's arm wrapped around her waist and hoisted Tasia to the surface, and the world, with its horrors and cruel noise, returned in a rush. She coughed and spit and fought Spiro as he dragged her to the shore and stretched her out over two flat stones above the water—it took Tasia minutes to realize who he was, that she was safe.

"Breathe," he said, climbing to kneel above her. "Breathe slowly, Tasia."

"A man," she coughed, feeling sludge—sludge!—in her throat. "A man in the tunnel."

"A man?" He glanced that way.

"Did he hurt you?" said Eleni, reaching the shore at Tasia's ankle. "Did he touch you?"

Tasia turned her head to the side, spitting the water from her lungs.

"Did you hear me, Tasia?"

She saw Spiro disappear into the tunnel. Tasia's fear was waning, a hard embarrassment taking root.

"I just got a little scared."

Eleni climbed onto the rocks, trying to comfort her. They lay there for a while, silently, as the laughter of the children in the pool resumed. Tasia's rasping slowed, growing less painful.

Spiro soon returned, Tasia's sketchbook in his hands. "There was no man," he said, "not even footprints." He placed the book on a dry stone far from the water. "How far was he from you?"

I couldn't say," she whispered. Tasia sat up gingerly, took slow, unsure breaths. "Maybe twenty feet."

"Vagabonds sometimes live in the catacombs, gypsies and the like, especially in summer." Spiro knelt, placing a muscular hand on Tasia's shoulder. "In the right part of town you might have found a whole community down there. But I never heard of them this near the center. Too many police to run them off."

"Vagabonds…" Tasia brushed wet bangs from her eyes, wondering where her ribbon had gone. "I feel so foolish."

"You should," said Eleni with a warm smile. "And learn to swim, will you?"

"Someday," she said quietly.

Fanning the hem of her dress to dry it, Tasia gathered her things—though she couldn't bring herself to go back in the tunnel to retrieve her chalks, nor rouse the courage to ask Spiro to get them for her. Instead, she shuffled home damp and depressed, Eleni dutifully trailing behind.

It was after supper when Tasia noticed the firmly bent page-corner in her art book, and flipping through, found the sketch, one drawn in her chalks, but not by her hand.

She gasped so loud that Eleni ran in from the kitchen. "What is it? What's the matter?"

"That man in the tunnel...the vagabond..." Tasia looked up at her sister, eyes wide as the moon. "He drew something in my book."

"What?"

"A heart."

"A heart?" thrilled Eleni. "A bloody human heart?"

"No." Tasia turned the sketchbook around. "A heart."

Мы будем всегда вместе.

# 6. Humble's Errand

Late that night, a bleary eyed Tasia sat in their parlor examining the sketch for the thousandth time, tracing the jagged chalk lines with her finger, wondering what sort of hand had left them and this note below:

*Мы будем всегда вместе.*

"We will always be together," she mumbled in Russian, a shiver on her spine even a half day later.

The door beneath the stairs creaked open and Mr. Humble emerged.

"Do you want to earn some money, Anastasia?" he asked in a wheezing whisper that made the hairs rise on the back of her neck as surely as that watcher in the tunnel had.

"Doing what?"

He glanced about as if the answer were some dark secret. "Where is your sister?"

"Upstairs."

"Fetch her and come with me."

Soon, Tasia stood with Eleni and Humble outside of the Odessa Brickworks, the massive yard a short jaunt up Grecheskaya Street and just inside the neighboring Slavic Quarter. The brickworks' rooftop clock, known to run slow to keep the workers at their toils, said it was a quarter-to-eleven, the great brick-manufacturing plant quiet as a ruin. No lamps were lit in the office windows, no figures moved among the rows of stacked bricks or ghostly white mounds of sand used to make the clay.

Mr. Humble motioned them to the fence that separated the brickworks from the street and pointed a meaty hand between the bars of the gate. "You see the window open to the summer air on the main building? That is the labor director's office. He possesses something that is rightfully mine. I want it back."

"What does he have?" asked Tasia.

"The details are none of your concern. But the infernal man keeps my possession inside a scarred leather case with a cloth handle. I've seen that case. Demanded its return fifty times to no avail. Bribes, threats, nothing moves him. The fool leaves me no choice." He scowled, his face hideous with tiny unshaven whiskers poking out irregularly from the ruined flesh. "Or better said, Anastasia, the fool gives *you* no choice. You two will fetch that case for me immediately."

"Fetch it? Us?" asked Eleni.

"You mean steal it for you, Mr. Humble," said Tasia. "Absolutely not."

"Yes, my sweetheart is a police constable."

"I can't steal what is already mine, can I, Eleni? I ask you to commit no crime." He paused until a horse and cart on the street passed safely by, then said, "Unfortunately, I am known in that brickworks from my frequent complaints. Had a row only yesterday. If I were caught inside, as an adult foreigner, it would mean police. An inquest. Likely jail time. While if you two girls were seen? Mere children trespassing out of youthful curiosity. They'd run you off with a warning. There is no risk—if *you* go."

"Never," protested Tasia.

"I'll give you ten weeks' rent tonight if you get that case for me." He jingled the coins in his coat pocket to make his point. "Do you hear the wealth, children?"

"Ten weeks…" whispered Eleni.

"It would ease your mother's mind, wouldn't it, girls? She wouldn't have to beg at the harbor. I saw her down there this morning, poor wretched woman. One wonders what else she does for money. A burden you can relieve her of. Just climb up the water pipe into the office and retrieve my prized case. The pipe would never hold my girth, but it could sustain little lithe nymphs like you." He held out a ring of keys. "You may need these inside. Skeleton keys."

Tasia pushed them away.

Eleni gripped the ring.

"Good girl. Always the wiser sister. These will turn almost any lock, Eleni. If the pipe denies you entry, try that side door behind that great pile of sand. The door leads to the kiln and firing rooms but there must be a stairway somewhere up to the next level. You want office 202."

"What kind of navigator has skeleton keys, Mr. Humble?"

"One who wishes to reclaim his property, Anastasia."

"You have nerve, sir," said Tasia, hands on hips, elbows jutting out to somehow look bigger, more threatening to their tenant. "Just because our family is poor, it doesn't mean we'll stoop to your wicked business. Eleni and I are not without conscience. We won't break the law for you!"

"Your sister disagrees."

"What?" Tasia turned about. Eleni had scaled the brickworks fence and was halfway across the yard, keys in hand.

"Eleni!" Are you mad?"

"Could be," she said without slowing. "We'll know soon." Eleni continued deeper into the yard and was soon lost behind a conical pile of white sand.

Tasia felt her stomach tighten in dread.

Humble laughed. "What kind of elder sister are you, Anastasia? Letting the baby go off on an adventure unchaperoned. Shame, shame."

"I'm only twenty minutes older," grumbled Tasia as she scrambled over the gate and hurried to find Eleni among the heaping manmade dunes, Humble cackling with her every step.

It was inky black behind piled bricks and sand, their masses cutting off light from the streetlamps. As her eyes adjusted to the darkness, Tasia spied Eleni standing beneath that opened window, a hand resting on the water pipe as she considered how to best climb it.

"Let's go back," said Tasia, tugging on her sister's free arm, rattling the keys in their tug-of-war. "I had premonitions about this place."

"I have premonitions too. Ten weeks rent." Eleni put a foot on the aluminum tie between two sections of pipe, pulling herself upwards. "But mine are after the fact."

"You can't have premonitions after the fact."

"I can."

"Come down!"

Eleni shimmied higher and was ten feet off the ground when her motion pulled the old pipe from its fasteners, the section crashing down. She landed with a plop in the mud, old rainwater flowing out of the remaining pipe to darken her hair.

"Ick," said Eleni. "I'm all wet."

"Little *fat* nymph. Can we go home now?"

"Let's find the door. We get the money, then we evict Humble. All in one fell swoop."

"If he keeps his promise."

They followed the building's perimeter through the yard, passing thickening brick piles and endless mounds of white sand collecting the Black Sea's moonlight. Some of the sand mounds were collapsed in spots, sunken peaks like miniature volcanoes, signs posted on their margins warning workers of sinkholes that drained the sands into those old mines, or the catacombs as the old folks called them. Odessa was as tunneled underneath as a block of Emmental de Savoieat at Madame Bellerose's cheese shop in the French Quarter.

They reached a lone iron door on a windowless building wall. Eleni sorted the keys, found one that she suspected might match the lock to the door.

She slid the key inside. "This one fits."

"Eleni, this is foolish," admonished Tasia. "We're not going in there. When Mother's absent I'm in charge!"

She opened the door and went inside.

"Eleni…wait!"

A gloomy hallway stretched out before them, enough moonlight flowing in to read "Kiln" and "Fire Room" on two of the doors. At the hall's end a stairwell rose up into darkness.

"If ole Henry-wife-killer had told us the nature of the job, we'd have brought a lantern," said Eleni, probing deeper into the hallway.

"We shouldn't be in here," said Tasia, just behind. "This is the evilest thing we've ever done."

"You spied on that lodger through the keyhole when he was having his bath."

"I did no such thing."

"Mama caught you."

"And if Mother caught us *here*?"

"Better she than the brickworks owners, Tasia." She jingled the keys. "Hard to be child trespassers with professional thieves' tools in your hand. I wish Spiro was here."

"Don't make so much noise."

They climbed the stairs to the next level. A long, high-ceilinged hall stretched out before them, three doors on either side, moonlight flowing in from an open window at the end. Near that window, their goal.

Office 202.

They were about to step out into the hall when the door to office 202 opened and a monstrous figure with a lamp in hand cast a terrifying two-headed shadow into the hall.

Tasia and Eleni ducked back into the recesses of the stairwell.

"The Specter?" whispered Eleni.

"The janitor," said Tasia.

Indeed, a man emerged, carrying a lamp in one hand and a mop—the source of the shadow's second "head"—in the other, while humming some old music hall tune. He left office 202 unlocked and entered the office across the hall, shutting the door behind him.

"Now's our chance, Tasia." They scurried down the hall into 202. Tasia closed the door ever-so-gently and Eleni slipped a skeleton key into the lock, fastening it shut.

"These are pretty handy," whispered Eleni. "I want a set for Christmas."

"Do you think Mr. Humble is a thief?"

"We're the thieves, Tasia."

The office was darker than the hallway, its window barely touched by moon glow. There was just enough light to see two heavy desks, assorted cabinets, a combination safe, and atop a high shelf loaded with books, folders, and chunks of clay and brick samples, sat a valise with a cloth handle.

Eleni scaled the desk in an instant, deftly pulling the valise from the shelf clutter without a sound or disturbing a thing. She retreated from desk to floor, kneeling and fiddling with the case's latch.

"Locked," she whispered. "Get the keys from the door, Tasia."

"Let's open it elsewhere."

"I want to know what old scar face is after."

Tasia grimaced, pulled the skeleton key out gingerly. As she did, another key entered the keyhole from the other side.

"Who's in here?" shouted a male voice as the bolt turned. "Show yourselves!"

Tasia pressed a shoulder against the door. "What can we do?"

"We jump," said Eleni, rushing to the window. "I think we can make the sand pile."

"It's two stories, Eleni!"

The janitor shoved his way inside, Tasia fleeing towards the window as he swung the mop like a battle ax. Eleni jumped first, valise in hand, hitting the mound hard, the case jarred from her grip. Tasia thought it opened, but had no time to consider. The mop-wielding assailant was upon her.

Tasia too sprang into darkness.

She landed at a different spot than her sister, her breath rushing out, the key ring lost into a sinkhole.

Slipping towards the same hole, Tasia found just enough footing to scramble over a sandy ridge to safety.

"What a day I've had," she said, gasping.

Eleni awaited, the locked case in hand. The twosome fled the yard as the janitor shouted above, casting his mop like a javelin to bounce harmlessly off the ground as they ran. In heartbeats, they were over the fence and away into the night with their benefactor, Mr. Humble.

Deep within the shadows of a Greek Quarter park, they at last paused to examine their plundered case.

"They won't find us here," said the huffing Englishman. "Give me my prize."

"We lost your keys." Eleni handed him the case.

"Their value will be subtracted from your payment." He withdrew a metal file from his breast pocket and began furiously working the valise's lock.

The case soon opened.

"Empty!" Humble shouted, smashing the valise repeatedly against a birch tree until it came apart in his thick hands. "You useless children have brought me nothing!" He kicked the remnants of the case up into the highest branches and pointed towards the brickworks. "Go back and get it this instant!"

"With the janitor alerted?" asked Tasia. "Do you want us arrested?"

"A suitable punishment for your bungling. Never send a Russian—"

"We're Greek."

"—to do an Englishman's work."

"If we go back and are caught," said Tasia, "we'll tell the police who sent us in there, won't we, Eleni?"

"And where he lives, too, Tasia."

"You girls wouldn't be so bold."

"What about our money?" shouted Eleni. "We got the case you wanted. It's not our fault it was empty."

"I'll pay nothing. Count yourselves lucky if I don't tell your mother her daughters are con artists and thieves! Cross me and there will be payback." He stomped off into the night, leaving the sisters standing alone.

Tasia sighed. "We need a second fell swoop, I guess, to be rid of him."

Eleni made no reply, peering through the trees as if to make certain Humble was gone. Finally, she said, "Tasia, the case opened when I landed on the sand mound. When I saw what it contained, I couldn't bargain with Humble. No matter the payment."

Tasia's dread returned. "What was it? Did it fall down a sinkhole?"

"No."

"Show me."

Eleni reached into her dress pocket and withdrew something white, narrow, and flailing at one end. In her palm was a small, skeletal hand.

# 7. The Hand in Hand

It was well after one o'clock in the dead of night, yet Eleni and Tasia could not go home to face Mother or Humble until they talked to Spiro.

Eleni claimed Spiro *always* knew what to do.

Tasia was skeptical. She did not see him with the same eyes as her sister.

"He sent you after a human skeleton?" asked Spiro, standing in the little alley outside his parents' house, looking over the tiny hand in the window light. Even at this hour his parents were awake inside, arguing fiercely as always. Tasia never remembered Mother fighting with Father before consumption took him. In calmer moments, she wondered what such a tumultuous home life did to

Spiro and if he'd bring such turmoil into a marriage someday with Eleni.

But at this hour, after this torturous day, she was grateful for his help and focused on the "hand in hand."

"He sent us after part of a body," said Tasia. "Though he never said 'skeleton' as I remember. Just sought an object inside the case, didn't he, Eleni?"

She nodded. "The bones are so small. Could it be from a child? Or maybe an old woman?"

"Not old," said Spiro, turning the thing over as he examined it. "No signs of arthritis or calcium bumps. But look at these drill points."

"Drill points?"

"Tiny holes in the wrist. Meant to relieve pressure on the tendon. Maybe its Paget's Disease. Wrist pain produced by daily handwork. Weavers, type setters, textile makers all get it. Even children if they've been workin' in a sweatshop long enough."

"How do you know all this?" asked Tasia.

"A detective friend told me. The Turks and Anatolia Greeks use these little drills on the wrists. Russians and English not so much."

"My sweetheart is so clever," said Eleni, nuzzling against Spiro.

"Why would Mr. Humble want this?" asked Tasia. "Could he be some kind of doctor? Don't they steal cadavers sometimes?"

"That's a serious crime, too," said Spiro.

"Your police beat takes you near the brickworks, doesn't it, Spiro?" asked Eleni. "Do you talk to the workers? Hear of a skeleton? Someone caught in the machinery? Or dug up somehow. Maybe excavating all that dirt?"

"No. The only time I was in the yard was as a strike breaker last spring. They don't talk to me much since then. Even the bosses since they lost."

"We should tell Mother. Evict Mr. Humble."

Spiro frowned, eyes shining in the window light. "Only if you want to go to jail, Tasia. This is theft. If you tell anyone, I can't protect you." He slipped the boney hand into his pocket, glancing through the windowpane to make certain his family wasn't listening. "I'll ask around about…this limb. Give me a week or so."

"We cannot have a monster like this under our roof for another week."

"How do you know he's a monster, Tasia? Did he tell you to retrieve a cadaver? No, you say it was only a case he mentioned. We don't know what he was actually after. Maybe he thought it was money or jewelry or incriminating love letters inside. How can we know?" He hugged Eleni closer, and with a free hand, finger-combed some of the dust and mud from her hair. "You two avoid Humble like...like he was the Specter or something. And keep on the right side of the law. Give me time to be the hero."

"Spiro the hero," Eleni said with a dreamy expression. They kissed.

Again, Tasia felt sick.

# 8. Jinxsy

It was early morning and they'd barely slept. The house stood empty except for Eleni puttering about in the kitchen, downing caffeinated tea to recover her strength. Even at this hour, Mother was already gone, down at the harbor seeking additional tenants, out pitching comfortable rooms to bed-needing sailors arriving with the first ships of dawn. Her absence thankfully delayed explanations about last night. And Mr. Humble had not yet returned from wherever he'd stormed off to after the "brickworks heist." To Tasia, that at least was merciful relief.

A knock came at their door.

With a sigh, Tasia rose wearily from her chair and answered it. Outside in the morning light stood a thin young man in his late teens. He wore a uniform resembling a bellhop or porter, though Tasia didn't recognize the odd emblems on his sleeves. The whole assembly—cap, jacket, and pants—was much too large, and hung in wrinkled clumps about his scarecrow frame. He smiled eternally like a lighthouse beam, a self-important expression on his freckled face.

"Hello," said Tasia to this curious figure.

"Hello, madam. I've a telegram for a Genry Gumble," he said, pronouncing the "H" like a "G" as some Russians do.

*Madam?* "We have a lodger named *Henry Humble*."

"Yes, that's him." He began to rifle through the bag at his hip. "Let me get the message. Who are you, if I might ask?"

"Miss Anastasia Karadopoulina. Our family owns this lodging house."

"Oh, good." He shook the bag, stray papers falling out and blowing down the street. "Where is that telegram? First day, you see, madam, just getting the hang of things." He peeked up at her, the way shy boys often did at Eleni. "Call me Jinxsy. It's a nickname, you know, born on Friday the Thirteenth, see?"

Tasia stared at the boy a moment. "Why would I call you anything?"

"Well, I might deliver more telegrams."

"You haven't delivered one yet."

Eleni came to the door. "Who's this?"

"It's Jinxsy," said Tasia.

"Jinxsy?"

"I was born on Friday the Thirteenth."

"Well, good for you."

He eyed Eleni for a minute, then returned to his bag. "You look like sisters." At last, he withdrew the telegram. "Here it is." He reread the front as if he'd forgotten the name. "Genry Gumble, is he in?"

"Genry is out," said Tasia, "but you can leave it with us."

"Oh, no. This is a priority message. It needs to be signed for by Mr. Gumble or a member of his family."

"Well, as I said—"

"I'm Mrs. Humble," exclaimed Eleni, plucking the telegram from Jinxsy's hand. "I can take it."

"You're his wife?"

"Yes, six months, like a dream. Where do I sign?"

"Here." He thrust a document and pen into her hands.

Tasia started to protest, but Eleni backed her into the door frame, then returned the signed form to the courier. "Is that all?"

"Well," Jinxsy said, extending his palm. "A gratuity, perhaps, Mrs. Gumble?"

"A gratuity?"

"Yes. A tip."

"A tip?" Eleni considered this a moment. "All right, a tip. Don't tell people your name is 'Jinxsy.'" She shut the door.

Safely inside, Eleni turned the latch. "We're getting our share of odd ones these days, aren't we?"

"'Mrs. Humble?'" Tasia crossed her arms, trying not to shout. "Do you think you'll get away with that?"

"Oh, he'll never know." She shrugged. "We're doing him a service. Now ole Henry will get his telegram." Eleni held the envelope up to the window light. "The flap's not glued, just tucked in."

"Don't you open that envelope, Eleni."

She opened the envelope.

"Eleni, don't you dare read that telegram!"

She read it.

"Eleni, what you're doing is illegal. It's immoral. It's unconscionable."

"You want to know what it says?"

"Of course."

"It's anonymous. No note of sender." Eleni handed it to Tasia, who stared intensely at the page:

FAMILY SAYS STOP KILLING NOW OR
FACE CONSEQUENCES!

"What does that mean?"

"I'll tell you what it means," said Eleni, taking back the telegram. "It proves Humble is not only a thief, but a murderer. Probably the Specter himself."

"How does it prove anything?"

"Right here in print. 'Stop killing.' They don't tell you to stop killing unless you start killing, do they?"

"Eleni, you can't just post a letter to a murderer and make him give it up. Do you think Scotland Yard wrote Jack-the-Ripper saying 'Dear Jack, you've been a naughty boy! Leave the girls alone'?"

"Don't try to be funny, Tasia. It doesn't suit you."

"Who's being funny?"

"This is from his family. An intervention!" She stormed out the front door. "I'm showing this telegram to Spiro."

"Eleni, I order you—"

She was gone.

Tasia sighed, stepping out onto the street to follow her sister. "Oh, to be an only child. Just for one day."

Spiro was not pleased. "Tasia's right, Eleni. It proves only that you two act without a thought to right and wrong. In twelve hours, you've committed two major crimes. You're hooligans!"

"But—"

"No more 'buts,' Eleni." He shoved the telegram into his pocket. "What am I supposed to do with this? I can't tell my superiors how I obtained a hand from a break-in or a telegram taken by 'Mrs. Humble' when you say 'Mrs. Humble' is dead."

"Then we'll find something you *can* show your superiors. Why this change of heart, darling?"

"I've come to my senses. Break the law again, Eleni, and I'll arrest you. Sweetheart or not."

# 9. The Draughty Courtyard

It was far too hot to sleep.

Without lighting the lamp, Tasia crossed the bare floorboards to her wardrobe, digging through the back to find the stocking containing her snuff box. Introduced to her by a Hungarian lodger last year, Tasia had quickly grown to favor tobacco. It made her feel more Bohemian, more the true artist to partake. As they must in free-living Bucharest. Or Paris.

Tasia closed the wardrobe, then, with a cautious glance back at sleeping Eleni, she went to the window, opened the pane, and crawled outside. So much to think about now.

So much to forget. Eleni had deserved what she got, but Spiro was so cruel.

Unlike him.

Nothing made sense.

Her bare feet gripped the rough slate covering as she slid down to a comfortable position on the roof, the familiar slant shallow and easy to sit upon. A nighttime breeze rushed up from the courtyard stones three stories below, carrying the assorted scents of city life.

Yes, she liked this. She felt both exalted and wonderfully insignificant sitting in the sky. Meditation was somehow easier in higher places.

Tasia pried open the snuff box, took a pinch, then sniffled, dissatisfied. *Old and flavorless*, she thought. How Tasia yearned for more money for the tobacconist, but she hadn't sold a drawing in ages. Maybe, if Mr. Humble *had* paid for that case, that human claw.

No. That wouldn't be right. Their tenant was corrupting them, by his actions, by his mystery. Up here, she felt purified. Tasia needed this sanctuary.

She slowly scooted down the roof, until her feet dangled over the edge. Freehand on the rain gutter, she took in the scene below. It was a typical enough Odessan landscape: a walkthrough courtyard called a *draught*, entered and exited by archway-tunnels on either side, crisscrossed with clothing lines and crawling with stray cats along the bottom.

The only point of notice in their courtyard was the tin-roofed wooden house wedged into the center. Surrounded on all sides by high limestone buildings, Mr. Telidis's home and music school reminded Tasia of a lonely cabin tucked away in some Carpathian mountain valley, the avalanche ready to take it at any moment.

Poor guy. He'd been there for—

The gutter's tin buckled and Tasia lurched forward. A dizzying view below, her grip instinctively tightened on the metal's edge, barely keeping her from tumbling forward off the roof. Heart thumping, she stared straight down into the abyss where she might have fallen…

And spied something unusual. A figure in a pleated cap standing in the shadows at the edge of the *draught.*

Mr. Humble.

With a long breath, she resettled herself on the roof, watching him. He was almost directly below her, back against the wall, midway between his window and the door to the kitchen, still as a statue, staring out into the courtyard.

What was he doing?

He took a few steps away from the wall. It seemed to Tasia he gave a slight wave to someone residing within the near archway, though she could see nothing in its inky depths.

He continued into the square, stopping at the edge of the communal water pump not far from the music school. Here, after some minutes, he pulled a cigarette from his breast pocket, then dug through his jacket, apparently in search of a match. As he did, a slip of paper fell free, fluttering down into the shallow basin below the pump. Apparently unnoticed, it floated on the surface for a few seconds before sinking out of sight.

Mr. Humble at last found his match, lit his cigarette, and wandered towards the far side of the courtyard, finally disappearing into the gloom behind Mr. Telidis's house.

Tasia waited, but Humble did not return. She decided he must have exited behind the house through the far tunnel.

Her eyes returned to the water pump. Well, whatever he dropped, it would be likely ruined sitting all night in the water.

Her curiosities reemerged.

Tasia scaled the roof, returning to her bedroom. She placed the snuff box inside the wardrobe, donned an un-seasonal coat, pulled the belt tight, and went down the stairs to the kitchen. Here she paused to peer through the window. Humble was nowhere to be seen. With a resolute breath, Tasia slid open the backdoor's latches, and marched down a short set of steps into the courtyard.

The stones were surprisingly cool under her feet, and she hurried to the water pump's basin. The paper rested on the bottom, its whiteness contrasting with the dark stone. Tasia pulled the palm-sized paper from the water, found it was two pages clipped together. Printed in English on the first page, handwriting on the next, she took only a quick glance before folding the wet pages and slipping them into her coat pocket. There were too many windows into the courtyard; she'd read it lat—

"Out late tonight, Tasia?"

She turned towards the familiar voice. It came from the shadows at the door of the music school. Tasia could see nothing under the roof's overhang, only the red-orange sphere of a burning cigarette held high and still.

"Mr. Telidis," said Tasia, wondering why she sounded nervous. "H-how are you?"

The burning ash said nothing.

"I just couldn't sleep, Mr. Telidis. Summer heat, you know?"

The ash fell, the toe of a shoe poking into the light to crush it out. "A lot of traffic through the square this evening."

"I haven't seen anybody." *Why did she lie? Was it instinctive at this point?*

"Hmmm."

Another pause. *Well, what now?* She caught a scent in the air, raised her eyes to the roof, to the fumes rising from his smokestack.

"What are you cooking?"

"Just heating a kettle. I always have tea before bed. Would you like to join me?"

"For the tea?"

"Yes, of course." He opened the door, the house light pouring into the courtyard. Tasia was surprised at his appearance. He wore a thin undershirt and trousers, shoes, but no stockings. She had never thought of him as muscular before, but he most certainly was. His hair uncombed, without glasses or that strange belt, Mr. Telidis looked far different than the man she knew.

"I think it's too late," she said, "for a woman to be in a bachelor's home."

"It's only tea."

"We'll have it at my next lesson."

"Thursday. The eighteenth."

"Yes." She tried to curtsey, but it turned into an awkward half-bow. "Until Thursday, Mr. Telidis. Goodnight."

Tasia returned to the kitchen, hearing Mr. Telidis's door shut before her own. She refastened the latches, stood there a moment, forehead pressed against the pane.

*The most boring Bohemian in the history of Bohemians,* you fool.

She shook odd thoughts from her mind, remembered the papers in her coat pocket. Tasia withdrew the damp pages, but there was not enough light in the kitchen. She moved to the parlor, opening a lamp at its lowest flame. Even in the dim light, she had little trouble reading the top page: a printed receipt for a purchase at "Loveless & Sons," 15b Mosley Street, London in the amount of forty-two pounds. It did not specify the item or items bought.

The second page was more difficult. It was a two-word note, handwritten in Russian by someone clearly not used to the cursive form of the language. The "r" was rendered in the English manner, the capital "д" all wrong. Probably made by Humble himself, she thought. Still, it was easily deciphered:

"Фонаръ Диониса."

"Dionysus's Lantern."

Now that, she thought, sounds Bohemian.

Tasia turned down the lamp, sitting there a moment in the darkness wondering what to do. The proper action, the landlady-ish course, would be to set them out on the table to dry. He'd be able to fetch them when Mother opened the door at daybreak.

Of course, he'd wonder who had found them and how we knew they were his.

Perhaps not, then.

She shoved Mother's big chair forwards, so it rested directly in front of the main door. *Ha! Get in past that, will you?* When he knocked at daybreak, she'd be the first to open it. Ask the "housecat" about his odd strolls through the courtyard at three in the morning. About signaling people hiding there in dark tunnels.

So Tasia sat, waiting as the minutes ticked away and she grew bored and sleepy. She made herself tea. When the pot was emptied, she went up to her room and retrieved her art box and began to organize her things on the sitting table she'd set by the chair.

She aligned her chalks and pencils, tossed her eraser in the air, thumbed through the drawings in the art book (skipping the heart and message from the vagrant), critiquing her own work. The distant clock rumbled five.

Where was he?

At last, she began to organize the various scraps at the bottom of the art tin: napkin sketches, childhood-keepsake scribblings, old ideas never begun, and the scrap of newspaper she'd clipped for the London drafting course the night Mr. Humble had arrived. She turned the clipping around in her hand for a moment, before her eyes noticed the fragment of review on the reverse:

than the Kardopulina Lodging home. All of the house's six rooms are equally
was domiciled on the ground floor. The simple décor was most comfortable, the
with a slight out of date elegance. Through my window was a view of a most
t courtyard, the charming notes of a nearby music school lulling me early to sleep
feather bed. The service exemplary. Mrs. Kardopulina and her two daughters
nmensely hospitable and trustworthy. I felt little hesitance in leaving my door

It struck her then that the full review in the English Club newsletter had quite a detailed and complimentary description of the bedroom Mr. Humble now occupied. The room he had insisted on occupying, never looking at any other. A room with strange creaks and cracks, a room which he seldom left, and then only in the odd hours of the morning, such as now.

He'd said he arrived at their door at random, hadn't he? Confused by the storm. But they'd seen him looking for street numbers. At least it appeared so.

When the review was published, what had Mother done? She'd gone down to the English Club and taken every copy they'd give her. She and Eleni had left copies in taverns, and wharf houses, and shipping offices, and a few museums and theaters. Even a brothel. Anywhere an English-speaking traveler might go. Anything, to get one more tenant to keep us afloat.

Could he have seen this? Could he have wanted this exact room?

Creaks.

Cracks.

Why?

Chin on her chest, eyes closed, Tasia was certain—absolutely certain—that she had not fallen asleep when she heard the invasive creak of a hinge. Her eyes flashed up to the front door, but no…it came from behind. She turned around in her chair to see the door to Mr. Humble's room opening.

"Up early this morning, Anastasia, aren't you?" he said, puffy-eyed and unshaven, shuffling past in his robe before pausing at the kitchen door. "Seems I never get privacy in this infernal house. Well, make me breakfast, girl. It's going to be a busy day."

The rumbling of distant Cathedral Clock told Tasia it was six a.m. exactly.

# 10. A Hunt in the Fog

"How did Humble get in that bedroom this morning?" whispered Tasia as she and Eleni stood in the expanding shadows of their courtyard at dusk. "The windows on the ground floor only open a crack. A cat couldn't crawl in."

"You must have fallen asleep and he walked right past you."

"He doesn't have a key to the kitchen door. And Mother second-bolts the front after twelve."

"Well, he got in. Either he's got more skeleton keys for the kitchen or he was already inside and you saw someone else in the courtyard."

"It was him. I'm sure."

"There's a third option. Underneath that rug…"

"I don't doubt it."

"This city's hollow with tunnels."

"Krek, krek, krek."

They paused to consider this, feeling the coming chill as dusk turned to night. Through the seawards opening of the draught came a drift of fog. Thin and slender, low upon the ground. But it always started this way in Odessa summertime. The haze would thicken and rise as the night went on. Some eves you couldn't see your hand in front of your face.

"Rather ghostly, this atmosphere," said Eleni as the mist seeped in.

"Well, he's taller than us at least. This gets higher, we can duck down and see him in this soup, but he won't see us."

"I think you have it backwards, Tasia. His head will be in the clear and *we'll* be lost."

"Time will tell."

They waited as the night grew darker, the air thicker. At last, a figure appeared in the opening to Grechsekaya Street. The fog to his shoulders, only the familiar scarred visage remained in sight above the haze.

"Humble," said Tasia.

They receded into the building's shadows, watching their tenant enter the courtyard. Unlike the night before, he did not tarry, instead moving quickly through the center and disappearing behind Mr. Telidis's house. The girls waited until he had time to walk a tolerable distance, then crept around to the other side and followed him out the opposite tunnel.

Under fog and shadow, they trailed Humble through Odessa. The Englishman avoided the wide gas-lit streets and moved via the courtyards, draughty to draughty, square to square, in a winding jigsaw path through the city. Bathed in mist, the Southern Wonder was now invisible but never mute. Conversations spilled from high windows, hooves clip-clopped on cobblestones, and the mechanical rumbling of trolley cars passed occasionally, the snap-pop of electricity on guide wires momentarily lighting up the night.

For at least an hour they traversed this shrouded world, their hunt made simpler by Humble's tendency to whistle as he walked. Often his silhouette slipped from their sight, only for the location to be revealed by his shrill siren.

"Where are we?" asked Eleni well into the second hour. "I can't see a thing."

"Near the dockyards. A rough area of town," whispered Tasia. "The newspapers say a man is robbed at gunpoint twice a week here."

"Well, he should move."

"Who?"

"The man robbed at gunpoint twice a week."

"Sometimes I don't understand you, Eleni."

"Obviously."

From somewhere in the mists came the mechanical chugging of an engine. For a moment, Tasia thought it a freight train serving the docks, fearing they were somehow standing on tracks lost beneath the fog. Then the dark rectangle rolled up near Humble at the street corner. He climbed aboard a commuter trolley just before it pulled away.

"We've lost him now."

"Here comes another trolley, Tasia. You got the fare?"

"Barely."

They boarded, looking out the windows as the city flowed by.

"It's so thick. We'll never find him like this."

"I know where he's going," replied Tasia, spying what she was looking for ahead, a sign in a window illuminated by rare electric light. "We get off this stop."

They exited the trolley, finding themselves in front of a teeming dockside bar, a boisterous haunt of sailors undeterred in their celebrations by the inclement weather. The electric sign of "Dionysus's Lantern" glowing like a beacon in the night.

As they moved closer into this lighted sphere, catcalls and offers of drinks erupted from the revelers inside. Tasia and Eleni retreated to a urine-smelling side alley to discuss their predicament.

"Looks kind of seedy, Eleni. Should we really go in there at this hour?"

"Free drinks. *You* wanted to follow him. Hey, look…" She nodded deeper into the alley. Tasia turned and peered into the recess. Illuminated by a half-opened side door, two figures conversed at the back of the alley. One in a dark coat, back to them. The other faced them, his face in the door's light. Mr. Humble.

"Can he see us?"

"I don't think so, Tasia…we're too far from the door."

They listened as Mr. Humble and his partner exchanged whispered words, one bit raising the hair on Tasia's neck.

"…murders are for show, only Nicholas's worth our time … Still, we carry on … workers recovered limb in catacombs … not good, incriminating…"

The rest blended into the raucous din from the tavern. Finally, the other man produced from his jacket an envelope and something oblong wrapped in a cloth. He handed them to the Englishman.

Humble unwrapped the bundle.

A small skeletal hand.

"The same hand?" asked Eleni, amazed. She took a step toward the men, but Tasia restrained her.

"They'll hear."

Finished with their exchange, or perhaps alerted by Eleni's outburst, the unknown man turned, passing their way intent on exiting the alley.

"Spiro!" shouted Eleni, shaking off Tasia's hold and rushing towards him.

"Eleni? My God. Why are you here? Did you actually follow me?"

"You gave our evidence to this monster? For money? You fiend!"

"You don't understand a thing. I told you to let me handle this."

"Traitor!" She struck him hard on the shoulder, but he ignored her blow and barreled out of the alley.

"It's over. And *we're* over, Eleni," he shouted over his shoulder. "I wash my hands of you."

Eleni followed him into the fog, cursing. Their shouts continued long after their forms had vanished.

Tasia glanced back at Humble at the alley's end. He shook his head sadly, grumbling a threat before stepping through the doorway into Dionysus's Lantern.

"Payback is coming, Anastasia. God knows I warned you."

# 11. Payback

After the horrors of Dionysus's Lantern, they knew Mr. Humble would waste no time with retribution.

So, neither could they.

Standing in her draughty courtyard, Tasia dug her fingers into the window frame and peeled back the wood. The section moved apart, separating right where Mr. Humble had split it.

"This was the cracking we heard, Eleni. Breaking the frame so he could slip the pane out and escape at night."

Standing beside her, Eleni pulled the glass free, setting the pane on the ground at the base of the house. They climbed into the bedroom, Tasia first, feet stepping down onto the familiar footstool against the inside wall. Tasia barely breathed, waiting in hushed stillness while her eyes adjusted to the interior light. The room was as it had been before, perhaps a bit neater: the bed made, the books arranged on the shelves and little dresser.

"He's tidied up a bit, hasn't he?" said Eleni, pulling herself inside. "What exactly are we looking for?"

"We'll know it when we find it. Anything incriminating your beloved has been sharing with him, maybe."

"Spiro's not my sweetheart. Not anymore."

The first thing Tasia did was roll back the thick Turkish rug. "Let's see what he's been up to under here."

The floor was exactly as it had been.

"Nothing, apparently," said Eleni.

"I hate red herrings."

"I prefer boiled cod."

Tasia went to the dresser and opened the top drawer. Inside were folded stockings and undergarments underneath mothballs and little else. She went into the cramped bathroom. The brass tub wedged inside was clean, its interior shiny as the day she'd scrubbed it spotless.

"Does he even bathe?" Tasia returned to find her sister on her knees, pulling a small red wooden case from beneath the bed, embossed letters on its shiny top.

"Loveless &Sons," Tasia read.

"Yes," said Eleni, working at the latches. "This looks like a gun case, Tasia."

"Mother specifically said no weapons."

"What about murdering people? Mama never said anything about that."

"We'll skip that part in the eviction notice. Open it."

At last Eleni got it unlatched. The interior was lined in green felt and inset with empty leather loops designed to secure a small gun. Along the inside edges were a series of empty indentations clearly meant for bullets. A small burlap sack was tucked in the base. Eleni unfolded it to find two eye holes cut in the sack's cloth.

"He's got a mask. Spooky." Eleni looked up at Tasia. "Do you think he keeps the pistol on him?"

"I don't want him here anymore, Eleni. Not with a mask, a pistol, and payback coming."

"Me neither." Eleni stood, placing the opened case on the bed. "Well, what next?"

"I don't know. Check those shelves by the window, the wastebasket, under the mattress. Maybe we can find that journal he keeps."

For a few minutes they wordlessly tossed and turned everything in the room. Tasia began to go through the books shelved atop the dresser. Most were the standards that Mother kept in the room for the guests: Homer, Pushkin, editions of the Bible in Greek and Russian. A Koran in Turkish. Yet, among these thick, rectangular tomes was a tall, thin, and unfamiliar book twice the height of the others. On its spine in English was *The Atlas of Odessa and Surrounding Environs, 1870*. She pulled it out, feeling the surprising weight of the book. Was this the most current atlas he could get? With all the construction it would be horribly out of date. Tasia opened it. Inside was the familiar three lion stamp of the English Club and hooked into the cover flap was an envelope nearly the size of a full page.

Tasia withdrew the envelope and opened it. Inside were photographs and newspaper clippings.

"Eleni, look at all this."

She came closer to peer over Tasia's shoulder. The clippings were from Odessa's newspapers, not just the major Russian journals, but also the Hebrew, Romanian, Greek, and Ukrainian, as well as a few British ones obviously taken from the English Club. No matter the language, the texts were heavily annotated, passages underlined in pencil, notes written in the margins all on the Specter murders: times of death, locations, and most insidiously, methods of killing.

And the photographs? Tasia felt a deathly chill rise up her spine. The photographs were the most heartbreaking, all young children, likely the victims—yes, one was the famous Polikoff boy; she recognized him instantly—all so innocent, with baby faces, unaware of their coming fates.

*Who could do such a thing? To babies…*

"There's writing on the back, Tasia."

Tasia flipped the one she held around. On the back was written 'Nicholas Polikoff. 11 June. One year anniversary of IRMS event."

"Look at this one," said Eleni, her voice cracking. "It's a mortuary photo. A young boy." She turned to the back. "'Killed fifth of June. Family: unknown. Surname: unknown. Vagrant.' How horrible, Tasia. No one to mourn the child."

"Poor creature. I'll mourn him."

"He's a monster, isn't he? Henry Humble."

"The Devil himself."

A metallic click caught their attention.

A key turned in the lock.

Mr. Humble walked in, eyes widening at what he saw.

"What are you doing in here?"

"We were cleaning," said Tasia, dropping the photograph.

He glanced about the room. At the opened files, the rolled rug, the newspaper clippings, the gun case on the bed. "Lies," he exclaimed, his face reddening, the outrage growing. "What gives you the right?"

"We were only dusting," shouted Eleni.

*Stay calm*, thought Tasia. *Don't escalate the situation. He might have that pistol.* "We'll all talk about this when Mother returns from the harbor." She nodded towards the door. "Come, Eleni."

He blocked their exit. "You're not leaving."

"Let us pass," said Tasia. "Or we'll call *your* policeman."

"Why are you in my things? What have you taken?"

"Nothing."

Tasia tried to duck past him, but his heavy hand caught her across the face, throwing her hard against the bedpost, and she tumbled over onto the mattress.

Everything afterwards happened in an instant. Eleni shoved him away from the door, but Humble trapped her arm in his grip, bending it backwards across her body.

"What have you stolen, you little vixen? Tell me."

"Let go of her." Tasia scrambled from the bed.

"I'll break it."

"You're hurting me."

"And then I'll break your precious neck."

*He'll kill her, just like he killed those children.*

Tasia seized the gun case from the bed and with all her power slammed it against the side of Mr. Humble's head. His grip slackened on Eleni, and with a hollow groan, he stumbled across the room and pitched forward to the floor, landing hard on his shoulder, and rolled onto his back, arms and legs fanned out like a youth making angels in the snow. He let out a low moan and did not move again.

Eleni fell back against the wall, rubbing her strained shoulder. "Oh, he's going to be angry when he comes to."

Tasia looked down at the case in her hands. Moist hair, bits of scalp on the darkened corner. *Get it away.* She flung the box to the floor. It thudded and clanked as it tumbled over the boards. There were sprinkles of blood at her feet, on her shoes, her dress.

Still massaging her injured arm, Eleni knelt down next to Humble.

"Close the door, Tasia. Mama may come home."

Tasia pressed the door shut.

Eleni placed two fingers high on Humble's neck, just beneath his jaw, held them there, silently counting, a dismayed expression on her face, ebbing towards horror.

"What? What is it, Eleni?"

She winced. "I think he's dead."

# 12. The Trouble with Henry

"Dead? He can't be dead."

Eleni nodded. "He's dead, all right."

"You just have to find a pulse. Old people...the, the loose skin, it's more difficult." Tasia knelt by the body, placed an ear against his chest. "He must be sleeping. I think I hear...no." Her fingers darted about him, pressing on every inch of his exposed skin. To the wrists, the throat, the temples, each motion getting quicker, more desperate. Finally, she ripped open his shirt, dug her hands deep into his salt-and-pepper chest hairs to find a heartbeat.

Nothing.

She looked up forlornly at Eleni. "He *is* dead."

"I told you."

Tasia rose, started to walk around the room in small circles. "This can't have happened. This is a dream. I'm sleeping. I will wake and everything will be okay."

Eleni continued through his coat pockets. "No gun. But there's a change purse, some chewing gum, a snuff box—tobacco?"

"No."

"You look like you needed it." Eleni found a leather card holder deep in his inside pocket. She withdrew a calling card and read it aloud.

"'Humble & Blackcomb Investigative Agency.' He's a detective." Eleni looked back at Tasia. "You've killed Sherlock Holmes."

"*We've* killed Sherlock Holmes."

"I didn't do anything."

"I was protecting you. He… Oh, God. Oh, God…I killed a man."

"Now, let's not panic."

"Too late." Tasia tightened her walking circles. "Too late. I'm panicking. I am most certainly panicking."

"Just because he's a detective, doesn't mean he's not the murderer."

Tasia stopped. "What?"

"I mean detectives, they see all the violence, all the bloodshed. It affects them, right? Eats away at their minds. They become just like the criminals they pursue."

"No. I don't believe you." She resumed her pacing.

"Mr. Humble was a brutish man, Tasia. And he lied to us. And kept murderous souvenirs. And why else have a mask? He must be the killer." Eleni got up, tracked down Tasia, and embraced her. "We're heroes, Tasia. The Specter's last newspaper letter said he'd strike on the seventeenth. That's today. When nothing happens, we'll know. Know that we got him."

"Is it possible? Heroes?"

"Heroines." Eleni smiled weakly. "We just have to wait."

*18 July*

*Those two last night were the easiest yet, dear friends. I told you I'd never stop, that my vengeful blade would...*

Eleni crumpled up the newspaper and threw it over her shoulder. "Oh, drat."

"What now?" asked Tasia.

"I'm thinking." Eleni propped both elbows on the kitchen table, lowered her voice since Mother was upstairs. "We'll need to do something. Have you salted him yet?"

"Is it my turn?"

"I did it the last three times."

Tasia muttered something, and then left the kitchen, passing through the parlor to the door of the bedroom beneath the stairs. As quiet as a mouse, she opened the door with Mr. Humble's key, slipped inside, and locked it again from within. The room was immaculate, the floor scrubbed spotless, and the furniture returned to its proper spots. Anyone glancing in would never guess the room's history. Or what lay behind the bathroom door.

From the bottom dresser drawer, she withdrew the bag of salt and went into the bathroom. It—she preferred to think of the body as an "it"—rested in the tub, *its* arms and *its* torso down, though *its* legs shot over the end. Eyes on the wall, she sprinkled the salt over the body, emptying the bag as she had done every time. There was no scent that she could detect, nothing rotting yet, the salt preserving him these past two days. She knew she should pack the salt down, press it into his flesh as Eleni had done. Tasia felt dizzy just thinking about it. No, she couldn't touch him, *it*...this corpse she'd made.

Tasia shuddered. They'd told Mother he'd gone to Kharkov for the week, but wanted to keep the room his own, locked and private. She'd even forged a note as proof. Humble's coin purse—*its coin purse*—had contained enough monies to advance Mother the rent and buy the bags of salt. Bags brought two at a time from the market every few hours. When the shopkeeper asked why, Tasia began alternating markets.

She threw the empty salt bag in the corner with the others, stepped out of the bathroom, closing the door gently. As she did, the air fanned out from the shutting door, carrying just a little odor. Somehow, she'd missed it standing there. The scent was nothing unusual, nothing worse than that found at a market, but it would grow.

Sight, touch, and now smell. All her senses betrayed her; told her she was a murderer. But they were nothing compared to her conscience. Tasia went over to the window, sat down and started to cry.

The kitchen door slammed, and a familiar voice shouted, "Eleni? Are you here?"

The girls looked at each other, stunned.

"Spiro."

"What does he want, Tasia?"

"How should I know?"

They rushed out of Humble's room, Tasia shutting the door firmly behind them. Spiro stood in the parlor in his constable's uniform, angry and red-faced. "What smells in here?"

"A rat died under the floorboards. What do you want?" asked Eleni with a sneer.

"Where is Henry Humble?" he demanded. "Your lodger owes me money!"

"'He owes?' Or 'Humble & Blackcomb Investigative Agency' owes you?'" said Tasia. "Yes, he told us *all* about his true identity. And his crusade to avenge the Specter victims."

"Not all of them. Only the Polikoff child. The rest were just dressing to disguise the motive, to make the killings look random when the killer was only after Nicholas Polikoff. At least, that's what Henry said. I'm surprised he told you; he was very paranoid about leaks."

"Why do you tell us now?"

"Because the bastard owes me for three weeks of leg work, Tasia. And twenty rubles for giving that hand to him. Another victim connected to the killer. I want people to know Humble jilted me. He doesn't walk in here soon, I'll go to the newspapers."

"If he *does* walk in, it'll make the papers too," said Eleni.

"Keep your voices down," said Tasia. "Mother is upstairs."

"So, I came clean with you. You come clean with me. Where is he? He's stood me up his last three meetings. I want to talk to him."

"He hasn't a word to say to you," said Eleni. "Believe me."

"He went to Kharkov," replied Tasia. "Three days ago. Following a hot lead."

"I doubt that. He said the suspect felt safest in Odessa, where he knew every nook and cranny. Every shortcut around the city."

The girls exchanged glances. "Who was his suspect?"

"Don't know. Humble wants all the glory of the catch. I'm just paid help." He stepped closer, his presence forcing Tasia back towards the bedroom door. "Or unpaid help. You sure you didn't run

Humble off? Send him on a wild goose chase with misinformation when he told you what he was doing?" Spiro glanced at Eleni. "Maybe you did it to get back at me, Eleni, for ending things? Fool him into skipping town without paying me?"

"Such ego, Spiro," said Eleni. "I haven't given you a thought since the day it was over."

He brushed past Tasia, turning the knob. "Let me see his room. If he's left monies, they're mine!"

"Never!" Tasia grabbed his arm as he tried to open the door. "Stay in here!"

"Get off me, Tasia!"

"What's all this ruckus?" asked Mother, descending the stairs. "Spiro, what are you doing?"

"Mama," said Eleni, "Spiro wants to break into Mr. Humble's room and steal things! We told him we'd never treat a tenant so thoughtlessly!"

Spiro released the doorknob, calmed himself, and walked over to the base of the stairs to converse with Mother. "Mrs. Karadopoulina, do you know what your daughters have been up to? Harassing your tenant constantly. They follow him at night. They read his telegrams. Peek in his window. Who knows how bad things have gotten? Henry's gone now. I think he won't come back from Kharkov."

Mother glanced around at all parties. "I don't understand."

"It pains me to say it, Mrs. Karadopoulina, but your daughters have become riffraff! The sort of hooligans I see in the street daily! And they ran off your only tenant. Ask them why!"

Mother's brow darkened at the news. "Are you here in official capacity, Spiro? As a constable?"

"No."

"Then I'd like to be alone with my family. Good day, sir."

Spiro glared at them all, storming out muttering, "Cost me a fortune."

When he was gone, Mother descended the stairs, and stood directly in front of Tasia, arms crossed.

"What has been going on with you two and Henry Humble? Where is he?"

"In Kharkov. Why are you staring at me, Mother?"

"Because you're the responsible one, Tasia."

"Oh, she's responsible," said Eleni. "I'll vouch for that."

"Hush. Well, Tasia? Out with it!"

"You see…Mother…we…were concerned…with Mr. Humble's habits…"

"We never followed Henry, Mama," interjected Eleni, stepping between Tasia and their mother. "Spiro is just jealous. He thinks I was—am—interested in that old man, accused me of trailing Henry around the city like a lovesick puppy. Didn't he, Tasia?"

"I suppose."

"A handsome boy like Spiro…jealous of Mr. Humble?"

"Yes, Mama. The rich foreigner, same old story. I think Spiro expected Henry to pay off his rival. That's what they do in Britain. You heard Spiro mention 'costing him a fortune.' And we most certainly haven't been reading anyone's telegrams. We promise. Both of us. Right, Tasia?"

"Yes, I guess we do."

"Another telegram for your husband, Mrs. Gumble."

"Thanks, Jinxsy."

Eleni slammed the door in his face and shouted up the stairs. "Mother?! Mother are you home?"

"She's at Agathe's, Eleni."

"Excellent." Eleni tore open the envelope and read the telegram aloud: "Two more killings in Odessa.

Polikoff family threatening contract termination. Bollinger enroute to assist."

"Another detective is coming!" moaned Tasia.

"There's no end to these Englishmen!"

# 13. Get Out and Stay Out

Tasia was sitting in the kitchen doing nothing. No housework, no art, not even thinking. She was incapable of any action. She just sat and stared and fought to keep her mind a blank. A tickling housefly crawled across her hand, but she failed to swat it. No killing anymore. She might not eat, not even plants. She'd starve, it was the only way to balance affairs.

Somewhere Tasia heard a thump, then some oddly regular clunking, followed by Eleni's voice. "Is Mother home?"

"No."

More clunking. It came from the parlor. "I spent the last of the money."

"More salt?" Tasia said wistfully.

"We won't need it." Eleni wheeled a large black baby carriage through the kitchen door. "We'll smuggle him out before Bollinger arrives or Spiro breaks in."

Tasia felt her eyes widen. "Henry won't fit in there."

Eleni set the carriage to one side, then returned to the parlor. "We'll do it in the bathtub."

"Do what in the bathtub?"

Her voice sounded strained in the other room. "It was terribly difficult getting these home by myself. Took forever." Eleni pushed another large carriage through the door, this one sky blue, embroidered with smiling clouds and flying ducks.

"What are we going to do with those?"

Eleni let out an exhausted breath, then rested her elbows on the carriage top. "I've done my work, now it's your turn to run an errand."

Tasia knocked on Mr. Telidis's door. Finally, he answered.

"Yes, Tasia?"

"Mr. Telidis, do you have a saw?"

"A saw?"

"Yes. Could we borrow one?" She twisted her hair with her fingers. "We won't need it long."

He looked at Tasia curiously with those spectacle-magnified eyes, then half-smiled. "You skipped our lesson on Thursday, Tasia. I was hurt."

"I'm dreadfully sorry, Mr. Telidis...I...I've developed Paget's Disease recently. Hurts the wrist to play piano."

"A common affliction amongst pianists. I know a physician who offers relief."

"Mr. Telidis, please, the saw?"

"One moment." He disappeared inside.

Tasia waited on his doorstep, feeling the warmth of the noon sun, and listening to the sounds of life around her. People bustled about in every apartment overlooking the courtyard, shouting to each other the local gossip from window to window. The usual housewife tittle-tattle, she thought, nothing fantastic, nothing too scandalous. Nothing like:

*"Where was that scarred Englishman today? I bet they killed him, Agathe."*

*"Who killed him?"*

*"That ugly Karadopoulina girl, the one with ribbons in her hair."*

Telidis returned, a large and worn-looking saw in his hands. "Will this do?"

"I think so."

He started to hand the saw to her, then pulled it back. "Bit of rust on the blade." He rubbed the spot out with his thumb. "There you go." He passed it to Tasia. "What do you need a saw for?"

"Household repairs." She shrugged. "Usual things, you know, uh, probably same as you."

"I'm sure." He tipped back the bridge of his glasses. "Well, no hurry to return it. I'm done with chores for a few days."

"All right." She stepped away. "Thank you." She tucked the saw under her arm and rushed home before the courtyard housewives noticed.

They wheeled the jittering carriages over the cobblestones of beautiful Italianskaya Street, trying to steer clear of the interlocked couples out for a late afternoon stroll along the acacia-shaded avenue.

"I think mine is leaking," pleaded Tasia.

"It's not."

"How do you know?" She bent down, looking at the carriage's underbelly. "It's definitely dampening."

"Lower your voice," Eleni said, pushing her own carriage ahead. "You thought it was leaking for the last four blocks."

"Well, it might be." Tasia pressed forward to catch up with her sister. "And I think we should reconsider this plan. I mean—the catacombs?"

"Where else are we going to put him?"

Tasia barely kept her whisper. "Don't you think it will look a bit unusual—two women wheeling baby carriages into the mines?"

"When we get to the park, we'll wait until dark. Then no one will see us go in."

"Oh, good. The mines after dark, that's just what—"

"Oh, no," gasped Eleni. "Mrs. Megalou!"

"Nosey Mrs. Megalou?"

"Yes."

"Where?" Then Tasia saw her. Mrs. Megalou emerged from a crowd of gabbing ladies on the walkway ahead, a trim middle-aged matron in a wide-brimmed lavender hat and a sunset sundress striding towards them.

*Arrogant biddy*, thought Tasia. Mother cleaned her house on Tuesdays.

"Well, it's the Karadopoulina Girls, isn't it?" Mrs. Megalou said in an affected Greek that didn't sound quite right. "Did one of you give birth, or are you the kind shepherdesses of others?"

"Shepherdesses," said Eleni briskly, moving away from her. "Of twins."

"Twins with twins, how amusing." Mrs. Megalou reached towards the hood of Tasia's carriage. "Let me see the little darlings."

"They're sleeping!" Tasia rushed the carriage forward out of reach.

Mrs. Megalou frowned. "Well, whose children are you minding? Can I ask that at least? And does the mother clean houses?"

"Mrs. Derko's!" Eleni blurted out.

"You don't mean Alla Derko had a baby?"

"Yes. Surprise to all. Well, must be going." Eleni pushed her carriage on down the road. "Goodbye."

"Good day, Mrs. Megalou," said Tasia, quickly following her sister.

When they were far from Mrs. Megalou, Tasia asked, "Why did you say Mrs. Derko had twins?"

"It was the first name that came to mind."

"Mrs. Derko is sixty-two years old, Eleni."

"I know. I know."

"And *Mr.* Derko died three years ago."

"Really? No wonder we never see him in church."

They waited until the park cleared out past midnight, rocking their silent carriages from a secluded bench off a little-used trail. Then they went down towards the quarry pool. The landscape was silent and empty, the trees smothering the breeze and light, leaving the waters still and black as obsidian glass. Tasia refused to enter the tunnel where she'd seen the watcher, so they found another on the opposite side, the entrance below the rusted ruin of an abandoned industrial drill. The carriage wheels caught in the dirt, but with effort they forced them through. The "no-admittance" government barricades inside the tunnel had long ago been hacked through by vandals, the odd planks hanging from the ceiling like wooden stalactites. Or fangs, perhaps, thought Tasia.

"Well, here we are," said Eleni, a slight hesitance in her voice. "The final fell swoop at last."

Tasia said nothing. She opened her carriage's hood and withdrew a policeman's electric torch, an unreturned loan from Spiro to Eleni made in better times. Tasia turned the cardboard cylinder about in her hand, felt its smoothness, found the metal of the switch, and pressed it forward. The night came alive with the strength of electric illumination: an impossible number of whitened insects fluttering in the foreground, the gray-brown walls of the tunnels extending into darkness behind.

And with a beam of modern electric light as their only protection, Tasia and Eleni Karadopoulina wheeled their carriages into the depths of Odessa's catacombs.

They were not alone.

# 14. The Labyrinth

"Don't you think this is far enough, Eleni?"

"People come in these tunnels all the time."

"Not down here." They were deeper inside the catacombs than Tasia had ever imagined they'd go, swallowed up inside the belly of the Earth. She felt constriction in the gray-brown walls around them, the air cold and devoid of oxygen. These mines had turned narrow in the lower passages, and they'd been forced to walk single file, Tasia now in the lead. She considered stopping, telling Eleni enough was enough.

"Let's just leave the carriages and get out and go home."

"Just a little further, Tasia, we saw footprints only two minutes ago. And an old campfire before that. We can't risk someone finding *him*."

"*'It'*…And it wasn't two minutes ago we saw the prints. A half-hour more likely."

"At most."

"At least," barked Tasia, though she couldn't really say as they had no watches. However long it really was since entering, maybe an hour, maybe two, it felt like her whole life. She'd dreamt of this deathly exploration before, down here with Eleni, though that realization had just come to her. Something in these tunnels resided in the recesses of her mind, hiding in premonitions and nightmares. But like in all her nightmares, she was never sure of the ending.

"If they find him, they'll hang us, Tasia."

Tasia's shoulders slumped. *No, Eleni, they'll only hang me. I won't let them touch you.*

Against her best judgment, Tasia pushed forward, Eleni right behind, her sister's carriage often bumping against her as they walked. Despite the dust and fallen stones, the floor was relatively smooth, the wheels little hindered. It was scarcely more difficult than traversing the streets above.

So far above, Tasia imagined.

"Eleni, if they hang you, do you think you die right away? Or do you feel something?"

"I don't know about hanging, but I once read a guillotined head can survive ten or fifteen seconds after the cutting. I wonder what they think about, rolling around in that little basket?"

"Enough about guillotined heads. I asked—"

Something walked across the tunnel ahead in the gloom.

"Did you see that, Eleni?" A quick turn of Tasia's torch beam revealed nothing but barren walls at the spot. "There was something there."

"Undulating haze," Eleni said. "From flooded passages down near the sea."

"It didn't look like haze."

"Breathe in. Can't you smell the salt in the air?"

"Yes."

"We must be at sea level. Or below it." Eleni coughed, the catacombs' seeping cold getting even into her strong lungs. "Maybe we walk under the sea bottom to old Istanbul."

Tasia looked up at the ceiling. *Crushed or drowned.* Nothing stands forever.

The tunnel turned suddenly black as the torch simply shut off. Tasia shook the hated cylinder. Why had they taken Spiro's foolish electric torch instead of a good old-fashioned lantern? The thing had a will of its own, flickering on or off with a frustrating randomness. At one point, they'd walked for at least ten minutes in pure blackness. A battery would never replace kerosene or wax for simple reliability. She cursed at it, and just as quickly the bulb flashed on, the tunnel illuminated. The haze retreated into darkness.

Tasia turned back to her sister. Eleni was smiling.

"I think cursing at the torch helped," said Eleni.

"What happens when this thing goes out for good?"

"We walk home. Very slowly."

Well then, while the torch did work, Tasia would waste no time. They pressed on. Eventually, the tunnel slanted sharply down, emptying into an expansive chamber cut out of the limestone rock, the dimensions too large for the torch to fully illuminate. Here, the cold salty air was at seaside strength, a slight sting residing inside Tasia's nostrils. They soon found the source, a green-water pool filling some sort of massive mining trough along the rear of the chamber.

She could taste the salt in her mouth. "The water must have seeped in here directly from the sea."

"I'll bet its deep," said Eleni. "Mining pits go down forever." Eleni rolled her carriage to the trough's edge.

"Goodbye, Mr. Humble. *Nos da.*" She sent the carriage over. It splashed into the water, righted itself briefly, bobbing like a cork in the water, then rolled on its side and with a gurgle, sank out of sight.

"I'll wager he won't write. Your turn, Tasia."

Tasia handed the torch to Eleni, and with a mingling of guilt, regret, and relief, she pushed hers forward. The water took it at the edge, the carriage floating out towards the center. But not yet sinking.

Eleni, exploring with the torch, shone the light to the near corner. "There's another exit out of here."

Tasia barely heard her. The carriage was just floating there.

"Eleni, it hasn't sunk."

"Maybe you got his bubbly bits. Did you weigh it down?"

"No, did you?"

"Yes, with stones before we left."

*She'd wheeled her carriage all this way with rocks in the bottom?* Amazing. Eleni was in fine shape. All that swimming. "Well, you might have suggested it for me?"

"I did. You don't listen."

Tasia looked at the carriage, sitting there like a little island in the center of the lake. What would she do if it wouldn't sink? She wasn't wading out there. Tasia took a few stones from the floor, tried to toss them onto the carriage. The splash of every miss echoed through the chamber.

*Drown, Mr. Humble. Drown.*

She threw another stone.

*Go away. We don't want you anymore.*

Out of the corner of her eye she sensed movement. That slinking haze again, strongest here by the water. She fought to ignore it—a natural occurrence, nothing to fear.

The chamber darkened as Eleni took their torch into an adjacent tunnel. Tasia realized how cold she was. She could just make out her breath rising in the air. *How can it be so chilly? It's summer. Were we on the opposite side of the Earth? Tunneled to Australia?*

"Tasia!" echoed Eleni's voice from far away.

The carriage was at last sinking, its black shape slipping below the water.

"I think it's under."

"Tasia!"

"Yes, it's gone. Thank God."

"Tasia, you'd better come here quickly!"

Certain that the carriage was at last out of sight, Tasia retreated from the pool's edge, following Eleni's shouts into the next tunnel. The passage was the same as dozens before, but on the floor were signs of habitation: layered wool blankets that formed a sort of bed, a fire pit carved down into the stone, old bottles and clay vases resting along the sides. On the walls, extending forever in the torch light, were large landscapes of Odessan city scenes, drawn in colored chalks by a hand with considerable skill. Recreating the infinite steps of the Boulevard Staircase, the sea overlook along Primorsky Boulevard, the wonderfully happy crowds enjoying elegant Deribasovskaya Street. All populated by city archetypes—the top-hatted aristocrat, the lowly peasant, the portly fishmonger, the carousing sailor, the humble Old Believer, on and on. But one figure among them was definitely drawn as an individual, a young woman in a long dress, residing near the center of every scene, something recognizable in her form, in the colors of her clothing…

"Look here," said Eleni, shining the torch beam on the nearest.

Tasia stepped closer to the drawing. That same young woman was kneeling on the grass of Langeron Park petting a small speckled animal—a cat, or perhaps a rabbit—while a man in a dark coat watched her from a grove of nearby trees. The face of her spy was so vivid, so striking in his lustful expression, that Tasia was amazed that it was formed by mere lines of chalk. He seemed as realistic as a photograph, more so, as if she could reach out, touch the voyeur's cheek, and feel the texture of his skin, the depth of his wanton face. And the girl he spied upon radiated innocence somehow, purity. And, more telling, familiarity.

"Tasia, it's you."

# 15. The Lair

"It's not me. It can't be." But Tasia's horror grew as she recognized the almond eyes, the round cheeks and narrow nose, the curly dark hair down the back adorned with purple ribbons tied in double-knots.

*The knots. He even got the knots right.*

"Oh God, Eleni, it *is* me." Tasia ran from landscape to landscape, scene to scene. Everywhere that same girl. "They're all me," she shouted. "Who could have done this?"

"I did," said a gravelly voice nearby. A shadow among the landscape figures moved, emerging into Eleni's torchlight, an impossibly thin old man in tattered rags, his skin ghastly pale as if never touched by the sun. In his grimy, curly-nailed hand was a wedge of pink chalk.

He drew a heart on the floor between them.

"I mean no harm, my sweet," he said, his speech gruff with disuse, his shining rat's eyes focused on Tasia. "I love you...loved you since I saw you in the tunnel...with the rabbit..." He swallowed hard, as if to summon his courage. "I need a bride. There are secrets in these tunnels. I can show you wonders undreamt in the world above. A whole civilization here!"

The girls glanced at each other.

Ran.

"Come back, my sweet. I'm...I'm so lonely! You will be happy here with me!"

They ducked into a new tunnel just as Eleni's torch cut out again.

"No, not that way, my sweet! He lives that way!"

In the darkness they sprinted on, joining hands so not to be separated in the lightless maze. They brushed against walls, turned corners to dead ends, and were often forced to backtrack, all the while listening for sounds of pursuit from behind, a phantom lurking close in the blackness. They could see nothing, but other senses compensated. The air's saltiness diminished slowly, indicating an inland route, and the path was steadily rising, the tunnels now closer to the surface. Their probing fingertips touched bricked passages, concrete slabs, and timber walls, frequent barriers separating domestic cellars and basements from the wild labyrinth. Happiness and normality lay behind those bricks. Sleepy families. Yet, a world away.

Eleni tripped, pulling Tasia to the floor with her.

Exhausted, they lay there, listening.

"I can still hear his breathing."

"That's me, Tasia."

"There's another rasping here."

"That's you."

"Is it?" She peered into the darkness the way they'd come. Or at least, the way she thought they'd come. Everything had turned about in their stumble.

"You wanted to date an artist."

"Not funny." Tasia turned her gaze the opposite way. "Look, a light!"

It was the softest white glow at a distance. They rose, cautiously approached. It soon became clear the light emanated from a sinkhole in the ceiling, one of several grouped together in this area. Drifts of sand lay on the floor beneath the ceiling, along with odd pieces of timber, rusted remnants of digging tools, and assorted garbage tossed or blown in. Through the largest hole, Tasia could see the brickworks clock atop the main building above, the time just visible in the early dawn of summer.

A quarter to five o'clock.

"Have we really only been inside four hours?" asked Eleni.

"We're so close to home."

"Mama will be cooking breakfast in an hour. She'll worry."

"Then let's be back by then."

They searched for an exit. Atop one sand mound protruded a small iron ring.

Eleni pulled it free. "Tasia, the skeleton keys you lost."

"Leave 'em, Eleni. They remind me of Mr. Humble."

She pocketed the ring anyway. Under the sinkhole of an adjacent passage, they found a discarded ladder laying on the tunnel floor.

"We can try this, Tasia. Help me lift it."

"There are rungs missing on the end."

"It's this or wait until the brickworks laborers come in at six and ask them to pull us up."

"And explain what we were doing here at night? Again? Maybe you're right, Eleni."

"Always am."

They raised the ladder, but the only place it reached was against the base of a trough along the great sinkhole's lip, a worm-eaten wooden barrier preventing a heaping sand mountain from slipping downwards into the tunnels. The ladder against it, the thin wooden dam trembled precariously, threatening to send an avalanche down upon them with the slightest provocation.

"Why is there so much sand, Tasia? Like a whole desert up there."

"You need sand to make clay. Clay to make bricks. The way Odessa is growing they keep tons in reserve." Tasia put a foot on the first rung. It snapped under her weight, the vibration releasing a drizzle of sand grains to coat Tasia's head and shoulders.

"Ugh." She shook off the dust. "Maybe not our first choice, Eleni."

"Or last."

They left this tunnel for another, the sinkholes growing scarcer, the passage darker. Eleni tried the electric torch, to her amazement it came to life, a pale-yellow spot on the wall ahead.

"Is this the way we came, Eleni?"

"No, I think this passes nearer to the Greek Quarter."

"I can't tell a thing."

Eleni shone the torch around as they advanced, the tunnel path rising again, the foundation stones of great limestone buildings appearing in the walls.

"Look at this, Tasia," said Eleni, bathing the tunnel wall in light. "Those base stones on the right are pinkish, those on the left a sort of pale blue-green. Just like Grecheskaya Street a few blocks from home. Where Mrs. Deveryanko has her boarding house, remember? And there—" She shone the light on a concrete column in the center of the passage. "This could be the base of the new telegraph tower they put at the corner. We can see it from our house. Our native Grecheskaya Street runs above us. We're almost home!"

Eleni ran down the tunnel, Tasia forced to follow or be left in the darkness. As she sped ahead, that flickering torch was little more than a spot of light in the darkness at times, an ambient glow around some corner.

"Wait, Eleni!"

When Tasia caught up to her sister, Eleni was shining the torch beam on a spot halfway up a crumbled part of the wall, thin boards spanning a hole.

"We're under our courtyard, Tasia. I'm sure of it. All those stones match. That boarded up spot must be our old cellar. The one Papa sealed up all those years ago."

"Those nails look too new to be hammered-in nineteen years ago, Eleni. Not a spot of rust on them. And the dust's all cleared away. And are those footprints? This is more recent work."

"Let's find out." Eleni pounded at the wooden barrier with the end of the torch. The brittle boards gave way, but predictably, the impact darkened the lamp bulb.

In the blackness, Tasia heard a shuffling of stones. "I'm crawling up inside, Tasia."

"Well?"

"I can't see anything."

"Is it our guest bedroom?"

"No. A storeroom, I think. Boxes and tools judging by the feel. Something wet and sticky here."

Tasia climbed up on the rubble, reached up inside the little opening, gripped the stone edges and tried to pull herself up.

"Help me."

She felt Eleni's hand on her arm, pulling her inside. Tasia got her torso over the lip, face and chest on a sticky wet floor, her head bumped against something.

Some sort of crate or box that shook with the impact. She pulled her legs up inside.

Tasia felt Eleni at her side, her sister's form shuddering as she pounded the torch against a wall or box, trying to will it into relighting.

"I will never trust electric lamps, Tasia."

Why was the floor wet? Tasia held out her hand, something dripping from above.

Somewhere near a piano was playing.

"Music, Eleni. We must be in Mr. Telidis's home. Thank G—"

The torch awakened.

A human head in their faces.

They screamed.

Then laughed in realization.

"It's only a plaster bust of Beethoven," said Tasia, relief washing over her as the little statue atop a box glared at them. "Oh, I hope Mr. Telidis didn't hear us shout, so embarrassing."

"Well, the music's stopped, Tasia. Bet he's coming."

"Humiliating."

Tasia glanced up at the source of the wetness. A hooded lantern hung on the wall, old, thick kerosene dripping down to the floor. *Better be careful, so flammable.*

She peered about. Yes, it was a storeroom. Shelves, stacked wooden crates, and small burlap sacks with stains on the outside. In the corner was a wicker basket full of rolled music sheets, works she recognized, had played many times for Mr. Telidis. The room had two doors: one at the top of three little brick steps that must lead to the house, and another open in the opposite corner. This door had many latches and lead to a tiny room with chains on the ceiling and stains on the walls and floor. It was otherwise empty. Now.

"What could he do in there?" asked Tasia, rising and shaking off the oil that had soaked her dress. She helped Eleni up, and was on her way to investigate this peculiar closet when she noticed something shimmering in the torchlight. Draped over a corner crate was a blue satin performance cloak, like a conductor or grand musician would don at a packed recital. It too was stained, and lifting it, Tasia read the inside collar. "The Odessa Conservatoire, IRMS."

Imperial Russian Musical Society. She'd read that acronym recently, hadn't she? Yes...on the back of a photograph in Henry Humble's notes. An IRMS event a year to the day before Nicholas Polikoff's killing.

Mr. Telidis had never mentioned an association with the IRMS. You'd think a music teacher would promote such a prestigious connection.

And these stains. Troubling.

Everything troubling.

Footsteps.

The stairs door sprang open. Mr. Telidis stood in the opening.

"Going through my musical society things, Tasia?"

"I...I'm sorry, Mr. Telidis. We got lost in the catacombs, thought this led to our house. I'm proud," she said, with an unconvincing tremor in her words. "I never knew my teacher was so prominent. The IRMS."

"Once prominent. Embarrass a rich family's child in front of an audience and they'll ruin you."

"What do you do in that little room?" asked Eleni with her typical bluntness.

"I'll show you."

He grabbed her and shoved her inside. Eleni landed with a thud and a metallic jingle. Telidis slammed the door shut and latched it.

"What are you doing?" shouted Tasia, backing towards the hole to the tunnels. "Let her out!"

"Did you find the termination letter the IRMS gave me? For slapping that brat Nicholas Polikoff at the recital. For his stumbling over Chopin."

"No, we just happened to—"

"Happened to break into my home from beneath. A day after a police constable visited you. Yes, I saw him. Spiro, isn't it? A friend of that English detective. What are you after? What did they send you to get as evidence? Did you use my own saw to break in here?"

She jumped down into the tunnel.

"We were friends, Tasia. And you betrayed me. After all the free lessons and lemonade."

Tasia landed hard on the piles of stones, something gashing her shoulder, the wind rushing out of her as she tumbled off the rubble onto the floor.

"Stay there, Tasia. It won't do you any good. I know this maze like the back of my hand."

Already on her feet, Tasia sprinted down the passage ahead of him. She tried to run, but her lungs could pull no air.

Why can't I get breaths?

We are not that deep.

Please, God, please.

A glance backwards. He carried that leaky hooded lantern, its beam shining right towards her. In his other hand was a silver pistol.

That lantern light flooded over her, her own shadows running ahead of her through the darkness.

"We're alone now, Tasia. As was meant to be," he shouted behind. "I wanted to try this pistol out since I took it off that masked fool. I only wish I'd given your friend Humble what I'll give you."

She heard a metallic click, then a shot. Something stirred the dust on the wall directly ahead of her.

Oh, God, oh God.

Tasia turned a corner, just enough ambient light off his lantern to see. In the path ahead was a fissure, some natural ravine that crossed the tunnel, perhaps eight feet wide. In this dim atmosphere, she could not see its bottom. It could drop five feet or five thousand.

She said a prayer and jumped in.

Tasia fell, the air rushing up. Then she hit bottom hard with a crunch, pain rushing up her leg. She held in the scream, though. Watched the lantern light grow above her. She'd fallen perhaps fifteen feet, maybe a little more. The earth was carved away here, littered with the spare dust of ancient mining or maybe the nearby brickworks. She pressed herself underneath the fissure's lip, crouching in the dust. Could she see him? Tasia grabbed a pointed stone, the sharpest she could find. If Telidis jumped down, she would send the sharp stone into his gut, or groin, or temple. If he shot at her with that gun, well, she was under the lip. He could only hit her legs or feet, only wound. If Telidis wanted to kill her, he would have to come down here, jump in front of her and give her a chance. One swing with her stone. One shot at him. Even the odds.

That glow grew brighter above. She heard his panting. Saw Telidis jump over the ravine, the lantern eye like a comet through the night sky. He landed with a thud on the opposite side, grumbling and complaining in Greek. Telidis moved on down the passage away from her.

Tasia held her breath. Thought of her sister trapped in Telidis's torture room. Could she find her way back to Eleni in this labyrinth?

The passage was completely dark now, her pursuer must be far from her. But could she be sure? Tasia got to her feet, felt the dust fall from her body. The pain throbbed in her knee and shoulder, but she hung onto her sharp stone. She moved on through the ravine, feeling her way blindly. The fissure opened into a wider chamber. There was the sound of dripping water.

Somewhere, something echoed. It was Telidis calling for her. As if she would answer. He must be mad—of course he was mad. He was a murderer. A murderer of at least eight children to cover for revenge upon one.

Tasia felt the jagged stone in her hand. She too was a murderer.

Let him come for her.

A lantern beam shone down from high above, her body in its spotlight. She started to scream as the sound of a firing gun echoed through the catacombs.

A hand appeared across her face, another forced the stone from her grip, and Tasia was pulled out of the lantern light into darkness.

"My sweet, I have you now."

# 16. Deaths in the Underearth

A filthy hand covered her mouth, an arm about her waist, he dragged her through the narrowest of passages, Tasia's kicking feet and flailing arms striking powdery walls on either side. But she could not manage to grip the sides or pull free a stone to use against her captor.

The man's voice was gravelly, but calm. "Have no fear, my sweet. I will let no harm befall you. We must spirit you away from the Lantern Holder." She felt his warm breath on her ear. "A wicked, wicked man, the Lantern Holder, who, like a creature of folklore, like the *bauk* of the Serbs, prowls tunnels snatching children from the surface."

"The same as you," she grunted beneath his vise-like fingers.

"I am not like him. I am good. You will see when we are wed."

Tasia kicked at him, but the man shook it off.

"The playful acts of love, my sweet."

"Let me go."

"Quiet. The Lantern Holder will hear."

As he dragged her on, light began to fill the tunnel. A natural light. Up ahead, stairs to an opening, the whiteness of birch trees visible against a morning sky.

"I am lonely, my sweet, but they say love must be set free." He released her at the steps, shrunk back into the tunnel. "I know you will come to me in time. And we will be together in bliss. As I have dreamt all my years in the tunnels."

Shocked at her sudden release, Tasia could muster no words. She rose up the steps, felt the sweetness of the air. The park. The exit in an old bunker ruin just behind Langeron Wall.

The wrong side of Langeron Wall.

Too long to get around.

She descended a few steps, in madness, back towards the catacombs she'd just escaped. Peered in at the old, tattered man lurking in the shadow of the entrance.

"Sir...my sister is trapped in Mr. Telidis's—the Lantern Holder's cellar—can you lead me there? Under Grecheskaya Street?"

"My sweet, it is too dangerous. He is out of his lair and angry, so very angry...like a *bauk* who grabs children to eat them. He will devour you."

"But Eleni..."

Tasia summoned her courage, sped back into the tunnel, brushing off the man's attempt to grab her.

"Come back, my sweet!"

She ran quickly, somewhat used to the game now. Think, Tasia. *What is the path home? It was a right turn...and then another right. And then a sharp left...no, a circular left...the colored foundation stones could help, if she had a light.*

"My sweet!" the croaking voice echoed behind her. "You must not—"

A gunshot.

She glanced back.

In a spotlight, the old man clutched his side, then slid down to the floor, and lay deathly still.

The source of the light approached. Mr. Telidis with his hooded lantern and smoking gun.

"Another rooster in the henhouse, Tasia? You disappoint me. I thought Eleni was the tramp."

Tasia ran. Trying to figure a way to circumvent him in the maze. To Eleni, to those stairs into the park or to—

She emerged from tunnel darkness into a region of daylit sinkholes above, sand dunes across the floor. The brickworks yard. Over her rasping breath, she heard the humming of gasoline engines and the voices of men. Early workers already at their toils.

As she emerged beneath a sinkhole, the men above spied her.

"Hey, it's a girl! You shouldn't be down there, little miss."

"Be cautious, girlie, that's not a safe hole you're in. The sand—"

"A man has my sister! Locked in a room! Help us!"

"What man? Where?"

"Near my home!"

A glow emerged from deep inside the tunnel, Telidis running towards her, pistol raised.

Tasia reached the ruined ladder. The second rung held. And the third, fourth, and fifth before the sixth snapped beneath her foot. The ladder's frame shuddered under her lurching motion, the end slamming against the sand dam, grains spilling out.

"Careful!" shouted another man above, throwing his wheel barrel aside to stare into the pit. More workers crept up behind him. "Don't move, girlie! I'll get a rope!"

Tasia clung to the ladder, the rung bowing, sand falling all around her.

"We got a child in the pit!" shouted someone somewhere. "Call the super! She's gonna be crushed!"

*Crushed,* thought Tasia.

"Here, grab hold of this," said one bare-chested man, lowering a thick rope towards her. Tasia wrapped it around her arm, but didn't yet have courage enough to step off the buckling rung.

"Tasia," said a cruel voice from below. "I've a perfect shot Like an amusement game at the seaside arcade."

She glanced down.

Gregorios Telidis stood at the ladder's base, the pistol pointed at her.

"Mr. Telidis…if you fire, they'll see you kill me!"

"If I let you go, they'd know anyway. This is fairer, Tasia. We each pay for our crimes."

She was doomed. But not Eleni. "He's imprisoned my sister! In the Telidis house on Grecheskaya Street!" Tasia shouted to the alarmed men above. "Eleni

Karadopoulina! Remember her! Find her after I die."

The men were casting stones and tools down at Telidis. He sidestepped a wheel barrel and steadied his aim, right at her head.

"We all go to Hell together, Tasia. In perfect harmo—"

Telidis was thrown forward, Eleni tackling him from behind, striking his skull with the iron loop of a key ring, like brass knuckles in her hand. The impact carried them against the ladder, toppling the frame, its end slamming against the sand barrier.

The dam burst.

The ladder remnants fell away. Tasia hung by the rope as an endless avalanche of sand slid past, filling the tunnels in an instant, burying Telidis and Eleni.

Choking inside a sun-eclipsing dust cloud, Tasia clung to the rope as the men pulled her to their level. One among them sought to calm her, but Tasia would not be consoled.

"Eleni!" she shouted. "Dig her out!"

Men wielding shovels scrambled over the heaping mound, half-invisible in the growing dust clouds, digging even as treacherous sands were still sliding deeper. A chorus of grunts, groans, and coughs as their spades split the dirt.

"Dig her out! Please, I can't see her!" Tasia glanced at the brickworks clock. At least a minute under.

Two.

Four.

Seven. "The clock is slow?" asked Tasia, begging for confirmation, fending off a woman trying to hand her a water tin. "The brickworks clocks are always slow. It hasn't been seven minutes?"

"Won't make no difference, dearie."

At eight minutes, there was a stirring. They pulled two bodies out.

Tasia couldn't look. "I won't be an only child, I won't…"

"She's alive."

Two men draped their jackets on the ground, and they lowered Eleni's spent, dust-covered form gently onto them.

"She's so still. Are you sure she's alive?" Tasia knelt at her sister's side.

"Eleni, it's Tasia. I'm here." She gripped her sister's hand, the iron ring still locked in her fingers.

Eleni stirred, coughing for an eternity before her eyes opened slightly and she whispered, "Oh, Tasia…it was horrible." She dropped the ring, skeleton keys flailing in the sand.

"How are you still with us?"

The faintest smile. "Oxygen debt. I told you. Nine children."

"We need to get her to the infirmary," said one of two men holding a stretcher. They eased her on.

"And Mr. Telidis?" asked Eleni.

Tasia spied the body nearby, surrounded by brickworks men. And a priest.

"Fellow didn't make it," said one.

The Specter was no more.

# 17. The Cycle Renews

A week later, sitting on their lodging house stairs, Tasia and Eleni watched Mother show a new guest the amenities.

"And this, Mr. Nuwar," said Mother proudly, "is the finest room in our house."

"It is perfect, Mrs. Karadopoulina. A second home."

"Anything for a lodger from London," she said, handing the well-dressed young Englishman the keys. "We had another from your city recently—a bit of a troublemaker—ran off without notice, but I don't hold such matters against all Londoners. Especially the barrister class."

"Well, I assure you, Mrs. Karadopoulina, you'll have no trouble from me. I'm a bit of a homebody."

"Call me 'Maria.' Your name isn't 'Henry,' is it?"

"No. 'Clive.'"

"Oh, good. Let's have some tea and go over the rules." They slipped into the kitchen, laughing as they went.

"He's no barrister," said Tasia when the adults were out of sight. "Not with such spotty shoes."

"Probably that other detective."

"Bollinger? Looking for evidence?"

"Yes."

"Better get rid of that saw."

"I don't know, Tasia. We may need it."

# ACKNOWLEDGEMENTS

The Author would like to thank the following kind souls for their assistance with *A Stranger from the Storm*: Shirley Bozic, Serhiy Zatsarinny, Yuriy Nezhura, Karen Keeley, Mary Adler, Olga Leshchenko, Yulia Tabatskaya, Katya Fedirko, Susan McCormick, Paula Messina, Steve Gardner and his family, William James McCormick and family, Ronald Linson and Deidre J Owen at Mannison Press, Drue Heinz, Hamish Robinson and the administrators of the Hawthornden Fellowship, Linda Landrigan and Jackie Sherbow at *Alfred Hitchcock's Mystery Magazine*, Martyn Bedford, and my peers at YouWriteOn.com.

# ABOUT THE AUTHOR

William Burton McCormick is a Shamus, Derringer, and Claymore awards finalist whose short fiction has appeared in Ellery Queen's Mystery Magazine, The Saturd*ay Evening Post, Sherlock Holmes Mystery Magazine, Black Mask, CWA Anthology of Short Stories: Mystery Tour,* and elsewhere. He is the author of the historical novel of the Baltic Republics, *Lenin's Harem*, as well as the modern thriller *KGB Banker* (the latter with whistleblower John Christmas). He is a graduate of Brown University, earned an MA in Novel Writing from the University of Manchester, and studied Russian history and language at Lomonosov Moscow State University. He is a member of Mystery Writers of

America, Crime Writers Association, International Thriller Writers, The Short Mystery Fiction Society, and was elected a Hawthornden Writing Fellow in Scotland in 2013. A world traveler, William has lived in seven countries including Ukraine, the setting of *A Stranger from the Storm*. He is enamored with the city of Odessa.

The characters of Tasia and Eleni Karadopoulina appeared in award-nominated stories in *Alfred Hitchcock's Mystery Magazine* and *Curiosities #3: Summer 2018*.

Learn more at www.williamburtonmccormick.com.

Follow William on social media:

Twitter @WBMCAuthor
or
Facebook.com/William-Burton-McCormick-365316520150776

# THANK YOU

Thanks for reading *A Stranger from the Storm*, a novella by William Burton McCormick, published by Mannison Press, LLC. We hope you enjoyed the story! Please remember to leave a review at your favorite retailer.

To discover more about William Burton McCormick and his work, visit his website at www.williamburtonmccormick.com.

To learn more about other Mannison Press publications, please visit the publisher's website at www.mannisonpress.com.

Printed in Great Britain
by Amazon

68663626R00102